Albert Réville, Philip Henry Wicksteed

The Native Religions of Mexico and Peru

Albert Réville, Philip Henry Wicksteed

The Native Religions of Mexico and Peru

ISBN/EAN: 9783337383176

Printed in Europe, USA, Canada, Australia, Japan

Cover: Foto ©Andreas Hilbeck / pixelio.de

More available books at **www.hansebooks.com**

THE NATIVE RELIGIONS

OF

MEXICO AND PERU

BY

ALBERT RÉVILLE, D. D.

PROFESSOR OF THE SCIENCE OF RELIGIONS AT THE COLLÈGE DE FRANCE

TRANSLATED BY PHILIP H. WICKSTEED, M.A.

[THE HIBBERT LECTURES, 1884]

NEW YORK

CHARLES SCRIBNER'S SONS

1884

CONTENTS.

LECTURE I.

INTRODUCTION. — CENTRAL AMERICA AND MEXICO. THEIR COMMON BASES OF CIVILIZATION AND RELIGION.

LECTURE II.

THE DEITIES AND MYTHS OF MEXICO.

LECTURE III.

THE SACRIFICES, SACERDOTAL AND MONASTIC INSTITUTIONS,
ESCHATOLOGY AND COSMOGONY OF MEXICO.

LECTURE IV.

PERU.—ITS CIVILIZATION AND CONSTITUTION.—THE LEGEND

OF THE INCAS: THEIR POLICY AND HISTORY.

LECTURE V.

THE FALL OF THE INCAS.—PERUVIAN MYTHOLOGY.

PRIESTHOOD.

LECTURE VI.

PERUVIAN CULTUS AND FESTIVALS—MORALS AND THE FUTURE LIFE—CONCLUSIONS.

LECTURE I.

INTRODUCTION.—CENTRAL AMERICA AND MEXICO. COMMON BASES OF CIVILIZATION AND RELIGION.

1

I.

INTRODUCTION.—CENTRAL AMERICA AND MEXICO. COMMON BASES OF CIVILIZATION AND RELIGION.

My first duty is to acknowledge the signal honour which the Hibbert Trustees have done me in inviting me to follow such a series of eminent men as the previous occupiers of this Chair, and to address you, in the free and earnest spirit of truth-loving and impartial research, on those great questions of religious history, which so justly pre-occupy the chosen spirits of European society. Our age is not, as is sometimes said, an age of positive science and of industrial discoveries alone, but also, and in a very high degree, an age of criticism and of history. It is to history, indeed, more than to anything else, that it looks for the lights which are to guide it in resolving the grave difficulties presented by the problems of the hour, in politics, in organization, and in social and religious life. Penetrated more deeply than the century that preceded it by the truth that the

development of humanity is not arbitrary, that the
law of continuity is no less rigorously applicable to
the successive evolutions of the human mind than to
the animal and vegetable transformations of the physical
world, it perceives that the present can be no other than
the expansion of germs contained in the past; it
attempts to pierce to the very essence of spiritual realities by investigating the methods and the laws of their
historical development; it strives, here as elsewhere,
to separate the permanent from the transient, the
substance from the accident, and is urged on in these
laborious researches by no mere dilettante curiosity,
but rather by the hope of arriving at a more accurate
knowledge of all that is true, all that is truly precious,
all that can claim, as the pure truth, our deliberate
adhesion and our love. And in the domain of Religion,
more especially, we can never lose our confidence that,
if historical research may sometimes compel us to
sacrifice illusions, or even beliefs that have been dear to
us, it gives us in return the right to walk in the paths
of the Eternal with a firmer step, and reveals with
growing clearness the marvelous aspiration of humanity towards a supreme reality, mysterious, nay incomprehensible, and yet in essential affinity with itself,
with its ideal, with its all that is purest and sublimest.
The history of religion is not only one of the branches
of human knowledge, but a prophecy as well. After

having shown us whence we come and the path we have trodden, it shadows forth the way we have yet to go, or at the very least it effects the orientation by which we may know in which direction it lies.

Gentlemen, in these Lectures I shall be loyal to the principles of impartial scholarship to which I understand this Chair to be consecrated. Expect neither theological controversy nor dogmatic discussion of any kind from me. It is as a historian that I am here, and as a historian I shall speak. Only let me say at once, that, while retaining my own very marked preferences, I place religion itself, as a faculty, an attribute, a tendency natural to the human mind above all the forms, even the most exalted, which it has assumed in time and space. I can conceive a *Templum Serenum* where shall meet in that love of truth, which at bottom is but one of the forms of love of God, all men of upright heart and pure will. To me, religion is a natural property and tendency, and consequently an innate need of the human spirit. That spirit, accidentally and in individual cases, may indeed be deprived of it; but if so, it is incomplete, mutilated, crippled. But observe that the recognition of religion itself (in distinction from the varied forms it may assume), as a natural tendency and essential need of the human mind, implies the reality of its object, even if that sacred object should withdraw itself from our understanding behind an impenetrable veil, even could we say nothing concerning it save this one word: IT IS! For it would be irrational to the last degree to lay down the existence of such a need and such a tendency, and yet believe that the need corresponds to nothing, that the tendency has no goal. Religious history, by bringing clearly into light the universality, the persistency and the prodigious intensity of religion in human life, is therefore, to my mind, one unbroken attestation to God.

And now it remains for me to express my lively regret that I am unable to address you in your own tongue. I often read your authors: I profit much by them. But I have emphatically not received the gift of tongues. By such an audience as I am now addressing, I am sure to be understood if I speak my mother tongue; but were I to venture on mutilating yours, I should instantly become completely unintelligible! Let me throw myself, then, upon your kind indulgence.

I.

I am about to speak to you on a subject little known in general, though it has already been studied very closely by specialists of great merit—I mean the religions professed in Mexico and Peru when, in the sixteenth century, a handful of Spanish adventurers achieved that conquest, almost like a fairy tale, which still remains one of the most extraordinary chapters of history. But I shall perhaps do well at the outset briefly to explain the very special importance of these now vanished religions.

The intrinsic interest of all the strange, original, dramatic and even grotesque features that they present to the historian, is in itself sufficiently great; for they possessed beliefs, institutions, and a developed mythology, which would bear comparison with anything known to antiquity in the Old World. But we have another very special and weighty reason for interesting ourselves in these religions of a demi-civilization, brusquely arrested in its development by the European invasion.

To render this motive as clear as possible, allow me a supposition. Suppose, then, that by a miracle of human genius we had found means of transporting ourselves to one of the neighbouring planets, Mars or Venus for example, and had found it to be inhabited, like our earth, by intelligent beings. As soon as we had satisfied the first curiosity excited by those physical and visible novelties which the planetary differences themselves could not fail to produce, we should turn with re-awakened interest to ask a host of such questions as the following: Do these intelligent inhabitants of Mars or Venus reason and feel as we do? Have they history? Have they religion?

Have they politics, arts, morals? And if it should happen that after due examination we found ourselves able to answer all these questions affirmatively, can you not imagine what interest there would be in comparing the history, politics, arts, morals and religion of these beings with our own? And if we found that the same fundamental principles, the same laws of evolution and transformation, the same internal logic, had asserted itself in Mars, in Venus and on the Earth, is it not clear that the fact would constitute a grand confirmation of our theories as to the fundamental identity of spiritual being, the conditions of its individual and collective genesis — in a word, the universal character of the laws of mind?

And now consider this. For the Europeans of the early sixteenth century, America, especially continental America, was absolutely equivalent to another planet upon which, thanks to the presaging genius of Christopher Columbus, the men of the Old World had at last set foot. At first they only found certain islands inhabited by men of another type and another colour than their own, still close upon the savage state. But before long they had reason to suspect that immense regions stretched to the west of the archipelago of the Antilles; they ventured ashore, and returned with a vague notion that there existed in the interior of the unknown continent mighty empires, whose wealth and military organization severed them widely indeed from the poor tribes of St. Domingo or Cuba, whom they had already discovered and had so cruelly oppressed. It was then that a bold captain conceived the apparently insane project of setting out with a few hundred men to conquer what passed for the richest and most powerful of these empires. His success demanded not only all his courage, but all his cold cruelty and absolute unscrupulousness, together with those favours which fortune sometimes reserves for audacity. At any rate he succeeded, and the rumours that had inflamed his imagination turned out to be true. On his way he came upon great cities, upon admirably cultivated lands, upon a complete social and military organization. He saw an unknown religion display itself before his eyes. There were temples, sacrifices, magnificent ceremonies. There were priests, there were convents, there were monks and nuns. To his profound amazement, he noticed the cross carved upon a great number of religious edifices, and saw a goddess who bore her infant in her arms. The natives had rites which closely recalled the Christian baptism and the Christian communion. As for our captain, neither he nor his contemporaries could see anything in all this parade of a religion, now so closely approaching, now so utterly remote, from their own, but a gigantic

ruse of the devil, who had led these unhappy natives
astray in order to secure their worship. But for us,
who know that the devil cannot help us to the genesis
of ancient mythologies and ancient religions—who
know likewise that the social and religious development of Central America was in the strictest sense
native and original, and that all attempts to bring it
into connection with a supposed earlier intercourse
with Asia or Europe have failed—the question presents itself under a very different aspect. In our Old
World, the natural religious development of man has
produced myths and mythologies, sacrificial rites and
priesthoods, temples, ascetics, gods and goddesses;
and on the basis of the Old World's experience we
might already feel entitled to say, "Such are the steps
and stages of religious evolution; such were the processes of the human spirit before the appearance of
the higher religions which are in some sort grafted
upon their elder sisters, and have in their turn absorbed
or spiritualized them." But there would still be room
to ask whether all this development had been natural
and spontaneous, whether successive imitations link-
ing one contiguous people to another had not transformed some local and isolated phenomenon into an
apparently general and international fact—much as
took place with the use of tea or cotton—without our
being compelled to recognize any necessary law of

human development in it. But what answer is possible
to the argument furnished by the discovery of the new
planet—I mean to say of America? How can we
resist this evidence that the whole organism of mythologies, gods, goddesses, sacrifices, temples and priesthoods, while varying enormously from race to race
and from nation to nation, yet, wherever human
beings are found, develops itself under the same laws,
the same principles and the same methods of deduction; that, in a word, given human nature anywhere,
its religious development is reared, on the same identical bases and passes through the same phases?

Mr. Max Müller, one of my most honored masters,
and one of those who have best deserved the gratitude of the learned world, has declared, with equal
justice and penetration, in his Preface to Mr. Wyatt
Gill's "Myths and Songs," that the possibility of
studying the Polynesian mythology is to the historian
what an opportunity of spending a time in the midst
of the plesiosauri and the megatherions would be to
the zoologist, or of walking in the shade of the vast
arborescent ferns that lie buried under our present
soil to the botanist. Polynesian mythology has in
fact preserved, down to our own day, the pre-historic
ages. And, similarly, the religions of Mexico and
Peru (for the empire of the Incas held the same sur-
prises and the same lessons in store for its explorers

as that of Montezuma had done) has enabled history
to carry to the point of demonstration its fundamental
thesis of the natural development, in subjection to
fixed laws, of the religious tendency in man. All
those curious resemblances amidst the differences
which we shall also bring out, between the religious
history of the New World and that of the Old, are not
at bottom any more extraordinary than the fact that,
in spite of the differences of physical type which
separated the natives from their conquerors, they
none the less saw with eyes, walked on feet, ate
with a mouth and digested with a stomach.

We shall begin our study with Mexico. But a few
prelimary ethnographical remarks are indispensable.
I spare you the catalogue of the numerous sources
and documents from which a detailed knowledge of
the Mexican religion may be drawn.[1]   Such a list is

---

[1] The second, third and fourth despatches (the first is lost) from *Fernando Cortes* to Charles V., written in 1520, 1522 and 1524 respectively.
Original editions as follows: "Carta de relacio*n* e*m*biada a su S.
majestad del e*m*perador n*ue*stro señor . . . por el capita*n* general de la
nueva spaña: Llamado ferna*n*do cortes," &c.: Seville, 1522. "Carta
tercera de relacio*n*: embiada por Ferna*n*do cortes," &c.: Seville, 1523.
"La quarta relacion q*ue* Ferna*n*do cortes gouernador y capitan general
. . . embio al muy alto . . . rey de España," &c.: Toledo, 1525. Recent
edition, with notes, &c.: "Cartas y Relaciones de Hernan Cortés al
Emperador Carlos V. colegidas é ilustradas por Don Pascual de Gay-

in place in a book rather than in a lecture. I will
only direct your attention to the noble collection

angos," &c.: Paris, 1866. English translation: "The Despatches of
Hernando Cortes," &c., translated by George Folsom: New York and
London, 1843.—*Francisco Lopez de Gómara* (Cortes' chaplain): "His-
pania Victrix. Primera y segunda parte de la historia general de las
Indias co*n* todo el descubrimiento, y cosas notables que han acaescido
dende que se ganaron hasta el año de 1551. Con la conquista de
Mexico y dela nueva España:" Modina del Campo, 1553. Also
printed in Vol. XXII. of the "Biblioteca de Autores Españoles:"
Madrid, 1852 (to the pagination of which references in future notes
will be made). There is an old English translation of Part II. of this
work, entitled, "The Pleasant Historie of the Conquest of the Weast
India, now called new Spayne, Atchieved by the worthy Prince Hernando Cortes, Marques of the Valley of Huaxacac, most delectable to
Reade: Translated out of the Spanishe tongue by T. N. [Thomas Nich-
olas], Anno 1578:" London.—*Bernal Diaz:* "Historia Verdadera de
la Nueva España escrita por el Capitan Bernal Diaz del Castillo, Uno
de sus Conquistadores. Sacada a luz por el P. M. Fr. Alonzo Remon,"
&c.: Madrid, 1632. English translation: "The Memoirs of the Con-
quistador Bernal Diaz del Castillo, written by Himself," &c.: translated
by John Ingram Lockhart, F.R.A.S. 2 vols.: London, 1844. There
is also a good French translation: "Historie Véridique de la conquête
. . . . par le Capitaine Bernal Diaz del Castillo," &c., by Dr. Jourdanet. Second edition: Paris, 1877.—*Las Casas.* Numerous works
collected by Llorente: "Collecion de las obras del Venerable Obispo
de Chiapa, don Bartolomé de las Casas, Defensor de la Libertad de los
Americanos." 2 vols.: Paris, 1822. Also translated into French, with
some additional matter, by the same Llorente, and published in the
same year at Paris. His "Historia de las Crueldades de los Españoles,"
&c., was translated into English in 1655 by J. Phillips, under the title

made in 1830 by one of your own compatriots, Lord
Kingsborough, under the title of "Antiquities of

of "The Tears of the Indians," &c., and dedicated to Oliver Cromwell.
[N. B. Translations in full or epitomized of several of the above
works, together with others, may be found in Vols. III. and IV. of
"Purchas his Pilgimes," &c.: London, 1625–26.]—*Sahagun's* history
of New Spain, a work of the utmost importance for the religious history
of Mexico, remained unpublished till the present century, and appeared
almost simultaneously in Mexico and London: "Historia General de
las Cosas de Nueva España . . . escribió el R. P. Fr. Bernardino de
Sahagun . . . uno de los primeros predicadores del santo evangelio en
aquellas regiones," &c. 3 vols.: Mexico, 1829–30. The same work
appeared in Vols. V. and VII. of Lord Kingsborough's collection.
Vid. infr. A French translation by Jourdanet appeared in 1880.—
Acosta: "Historia Natural y Moral de las Indias . . . compuesta por
el Padre Joseph de Acosta Religioso de la Campañia de Jesus," &c.:
Seville, 1590. English translation: "The Naturall and Morall His-
torie of the East and West Indies," &c.: translated by E. G.: London,
1604. Edward Grimstone's translation was edited, with notes, for the
Hakluyt Society, by Clements R. Markham, in 1880.—*Torquemada:*
"Los veynte y un libros Rituales y Monarchia Yndiana . . . Compuesto
por Fray Ivan de Torquemanda," &c. 3 vols.: Seville, 1615. Printed
again at Madrid in 1723.—*Herrera* (official historiographer of Philip
II.) : "Historia General de los Hechos de los Castellanos en las Islas i
Tierra Firme del mar Oceano," &c., by Antonio de Herrera; to which
is prefixed, "Descripcion de las Indias Ocidentales," &c., by the same.
4 vols.: Madrid, 1601. English translation in epitome by Capt. John
Stevens, "The General History of the vast Continent and Islands of
America," &c. 6 vols. : London, 1725–26.

The following native writers may also be consulted. *Ixtlilxochitl*
(Fernando de Alva) : "Historia Chichimeca" and "Relaciones," in
Lord Kingsborough's "Mexican Antiquities," Vol. IX. (vid. infr.).
French translations in Vols. VIII. XII. and XIII. of H. Ternaux-

Mexico," a work of extreme importance, which reproduces in facsimile or engravings, the monuments

Compans' collection: "Voyages, Relations et Memoires originaux pour servir a l'histoire de la Découverte de l'Amérique:" Paris, 1837-41.—*Camargo:* "Histoire de la République de Tlaxcallan, par Domingo Muñoz Camargo, Indien, natif de cette ville," translated from the Spanish MS. in Vols. XCVIII. and XCIX. of the "Nouvelles Annales des Voyages," &c.: Paris, 1843.—*Pomar (J. B. de):* "Relacion de las Antiquedades de los Indios." Pomar was a descendant of the royal house of Tezcuco, and his memoirs were made use of in MS. by Torquemada.

Amongst later authorities may be mentioned (in addition to Prescott's well-known work, and those cited in the following notes): *W. Robertson:* "History of America."—*Alx. von Humboldt:* "Vues des Cordillières et Monuments des peuples de l'Amérique:" Paris, 1810; forming the "Atlas Pittoresque" of Part III. of "Voyage de Humboldt et Bonpland."—*Francesco Saverio Clavigero:* "Storia antica del Messico," &c. 4 vols.: Cesena, 1780-81. English translation by Charles Cullen: "The History of Mexico," &c. 2 vols.: London, 1787.—*Th. Waitz:* "Anthropologie der Naturvölker," Vol. IV.: Leipzig, 1864.—*Brasseur de Bourbourg:* "Histoire des Nations civilisées du Mexique et de L'Amérique-centrale," &c. 4 vols: Paris, 1857-59.—*Müller (Joh. George),* Professor at Bâle: "Geschichte der Amerikanischen Urreligionen." Second edition: Basel, 1867.—To these should be added the narratives and works of M. *D. Charnay,* still in the course of publication.

References will be given to the originals, but in such a form, wherever possible, as to serve equally well for the English and French translations. Where, as is not unfrequently the case, the chapters or sections of the translations do not correspond to the originals, a note of the vol. and page of the former will generally be added.

and ruins of ancient Mexico;[1] and the very remarkable work of Mr. H. H. Bancroft, "Native Races of the Pacific States of North America."[2]

II.

The region with which we are now to occupy ourselves comprises the space bounded on the South by the Isthmus of Panama, washed East and West by the oceans, and determined, roughly speaking, towards the North by a line starting from the head of the Gulf of California, and sweeping round to the mouths of the Mississippi with a curve that takes in Arizona and Southern Texas. In our day, this southern portion of North America is broken into two great divisions, the first and most southern of which is known collectively as Central America, and embraces the republics of Guatemala, Honduras, Nicaragua, Costa Rica, San Salvador and Panama. The great peninsula of Yucatan, which is now Mexican,

[1] The original collection is in seven magnificent folio volumes. "Antiquities of Mexico: comprising Facsimiles of Ancient Mexican Paintings and Hieroglyphics . . . together with The Monuments of New Spain, by M. Dupaix . . . the whole illustrated by many valuable inedited Manuscripts by Augustine Aglio:" London, 1830. Two supplementary volumes, on the title-page of which Lord Kingsborough's own name appears, were added in 1848, and a tenth volume was projected, but only a small portion of it (appended to Vol. IX.) was printed.

[2] Five volumes: New York, 1875–76.

formerly belonged to this group of Central American peoples. The second portion of the territory we are to study corresponds to the present republic of Mexico. I shall presently explain the sense in which it might be called the Mexican empire in the time of Fernando Cortes. For the present, let me ask you to remember that we are now about to speak, in a general and preliminary manner, of the region which pretty closely corresponds to the present Central America and Mexico.

To begin with, we treat these two districts as a single whole, because the Europeans found them inhabited by a race which was divided, it is true, into several varieties, but was distinguished clearly from the Red-skins on the North, and still more from the Eskimos, and alone of the native races of North America had proved itself capable of rising by its own strength to a veritable civilization. The general physical type of the race is marked by a very brown skin, a medium stature, low brow, black coarse hair, prominent jaw, heavy lips, thick eye-brows, and a nose generally large and often hooked. The noble families as a rule had a clearer complexion. The women are thick-set and squab, but not without grace in their movements. In their youth they are sometimes very pretty, but they fade early. We must leave it to ethnological specialists to decide whether this type is not the result of previous crossings.

B

So much is certain, that at an epoch the date of
which it is impossible to fix, but which must have
been remote, this race, cut off from all the world by
the sea and the profoundest savagery, developed a
civilization *sui generis*, to which the traditional reminiscences of the natives and a series of most remarkable
ruins, discovered especially in Central America, bear
witness.   For it is in this southern district that we
find the monumental ruins of Palenque, of Chiapa, of
Uxmal, of Utatlan, and of other places, the list of
which has again begun to receive additions in recent
years.   When the Spaniards conquered the New
World, the centre of this civilization had shifted further north, to Mexico proper, to the city of Mexico,
to Tezcuco and to Cholula.   But the consciousness
that the Mexican civilization was affiliated to that of
the isthmic region had by no means been lost.   It
was a nation or race called Maya, the name of which
seems to indicate that it considered itself indigenous,
and the proper centre of which lay in Yucatan, that produced this American civilization—capable of organizing states and priesthoods, of rearing immense palaces,
of carving stone in great perfection and with a true
artistic sense, and of realizing a high degree of physical
well-being.   There is reason to believe, however, that
this civilization, resembling in some respects that of
ancient Canaan, had more refinement in its pursuit of

material comfort than vigour in its morality. A certain effeminacy, and even the endemic practice of odious vices, appears to have early enervated it. When the Spaniards arrived in America, wars and devastating invasions had shattered the old and powerful monarchies of the central region and reduced the great monuments of antiquity to ruins, and that too so long ago that the natives themselves, while retaining a certain civilization, had lost all memory of the ancient cities and the ancient palaces that the Europeans rescued from oblivion. We may still see figured amongst the monuments of Mexico those beautiful ruins of Palenque, where stretches a superb gallery, vaulted with the broad ogives that recall the Moorish architecture of the Alhambra; while at Tehuantepec an immense temple has been discovered, hollowed out of a huge rock, like certain temples in India. The cultivation of maize was to this region what that of wheat was to Egypt and Mesopotamia, or of rice to India and China, the material condition, namely, of a precocious civilization. For, as has been remarked, the primitive civilizations could not be developed except where an abundant cereal raised man above immediate anxiety for his subsistence, and rescued him from the all-engrossing fatigues and the dangerous uncertainties of the hunter's life.

This Maya race, having adopted the agricultural

and sedentary life, multiplied so greatly as to send out
many swarms of colonists towards the North, where
the *Nahuas*, that is to say, "the skilled ones" or
"experts" (for so the emigrants from the Maya land
were called), found men of the same race as themselves, to whom they imparted their superior knowledge. They kept on pushing northwards, established
themselves on the great plateau of Anahuac, or "lake
country," where the city of Mexico is situated, and
advanced up to the somewhat indefinite limit opposed
to their progress by the Redskins. This migratory
movement towards the North was evidently not the
affair of a day. It must have continued for centuries;
and during its process the Maya civilization may have
experienced great developments and undergone numerous modifications; so that, without venturing to pronounce categorically upon a problem yet unsolved, I
should myself be inclined to ascribe to a population,
which either consisted of bands of emigrant Mayas or
was affected by this Nahua movement, those "Mounds"
which still throw their galling defiance at the modern
methods of research, powerless to explain their origin
in regions which have since been under the reign of
the most absolute savagery.

However this may be, the movement by which in a
remote antiquity the peoples of Central America
ascended towards the North, carrying with them their

relative civilization to Mexico and even beyond, was reversed at the epoch of our Middle Ages by a migration in the opposite direction. In this case it was the peoples of the northern regions that tended to beat back upon the South. They invaded, conquered and brought into·subjection the peoples who had established themselves along the path followed by the previous migrations ; and it is probably to invasions of this description that we must ascribe the fall of the ancient Maya society of the isthmic region. But the civilization of which it had sown the germs was not dead. Nay, the peoples who descended upon the South had in great measure themselves adopted it ; and in the invaded districts there remained groups and nuclei of Nahua populations who maintained its principles, its arts and its spirit, to which their conquerors readily conformed. The last conquerors had been established as masters in the Mexican district for more than a century when the Spaniards arrived there. They were the *Aztecs.* They had conquered or shattered what was called the *Chichimec* empire, which in its turn had destroyed, some centuries earlier, the *Toltec* empire. But it would be a mistake to think of three successive empires, Toltec, Chichimec and Aztec, one supplanting the other in the same way as the Frankish empire, for example, took the place of that of Rome, which in its turn had replaced divers others more

ancient yet. What really took place was what
follows.

The prolonged migrations of the Nahuas towards the
North had not spread civilization uniformly amongst
all the tribes encountered on the route. Thus, down
to the sixteenth century, there still existed in the heart
of Mexico tribes very little removed from the savage
state, such as the Otomis or " wanderers ;" whereas, in
other districts, the Nahuas had established themselves
on a footing of acknowledged supremacy and developed a brilliant civilization. Thus they founded at the
extreme north of the present Mexico the ancient city
of Tulan or Tullan, the name of which passed into
that of its inhabitants, the *Toltecs*, and this latter, in its
turn, became the designation of everything graceful,
elegant, artistically refined and beautiful. Ethnogra-
phically, it simply indicates the most brilliant foci of
the civilization imported from Central America. In
fact there never was a Toltec empire at all, but simply
a confederation of the three cities of Tullan, Colhua-
can and Otompan, all of which may be regarded as
Toltec in the social sense which I have just described.
Many other small states existed outside this confederation. It was destroyed by the revolt or invasion of
more northern tribes, hitherto held in vassalage and
looked down upon as belonging to a lower level of
culture and manners. These tribes received or assumed

the name of *Chichimecs* or "dogs," which may have
been a term of contempt converted into a title of
honour, like that of the *Gueux* of the Low Countries.
Thus arose a Chichimec confederation, of which Col-
huacan (the name given for a time to Tezcuco), Azca-
pulzalco, the capital of the Tepanecs, and Tlacopan,
were the principal cities. At Tezcuco the Toltec element was still powerful. Cholula, a sacred city,
remained essentially Toltec, and in general the Chichimecs readily adopted the superior civilization of
the Toltecs. This was so much the case that Tezcuco
became the seat of an intellectual and artistic development, in virtue of which the Europeans called it the
Athens of Mexico. It was from the eleventh to the
fourteenth centuries, according to the historians, that
what may be called the Chichimec era lasted.

At the beginning of the fifteenth century, the Aztecs
—that is to say *the white flamingos* or *herons* (from
aztatl), the last comers from the North, who had long
been a poor and wretched tribe, and on reaching Anahuac had been obliged to accept the suzerainty of
Tezcuco—began to assume great importance. They
had founded, under the name of Tenochtitlan, upon an
island that is now united to the mainland, the city
which was afterwards called Mexico. But originally
the name of Mexico belonged to the quarter of the
city which was dedicated to the God of war Mextli.

At once warlike and commercial, the Aztecs grew in numbers, wealth and military power; they saved Tezcuco from the dominion of the Tepanecs, who tried to bring the whole Chichimec confederation into subjection; presently they threw off all vassalage, and in the fifteenth century they stood at the head of the new confederation which took the place of that of the Chichimecs, and of which Mexico, Tezcuco and Tlacopan (or Tacuba), were the three capitals.

There was no Mexican empire, then, at the moment when Fernando Cortes disembarked near Vera Cruz, but there was a federation. On certain days of religious festivity a solemn public dance was celebrated in Mexico, in which the sovereign families of the three states, together with their subjects of the highest rank, took part. It began at noon before the palace of the Mexican king. They stood three and three. The king of Mexico led the dance, holding with his right hand the king of Tezcuco, and with his left the king of Tlacopan, and the three confederate sovereigns or emperors thus symbolized for several hours the union of their three states by the harmonious cadence of their movements.[1]

III.

The widely-spread error that makes Montezuma, the Mexican sovereign that received Fernando Cortes,

[1] See *Bancroft*, Vol. II. pp. 311, 312.

the absolute master of the whole district of the present
Mexico, is explained by the fact, that of the three confederate states that of the Aztecs was by far the
strongest, most warlike and most dreaded. It was
constantly extending its dominion by means of a
numerous, disciplined and admirably organized army,
and little by little the other two states were constantly
approaching the condition of vassalage. The Aztecs
were no more recalcitrant to civilization than the
Chichimecs, but they were ruder, more matter-of-fact
and more cruel. They did no sacrifices to the Toltec
graces, but developed their civilization exclusively on
its utilitarian and practical side. They were no artists,
but essentially warriors and merchants. And even
their merchants were often at the same time spies
whom the kings of Mexico sent into the countries they
coveted, to study their resources, their strength and
their weakness. Their yoke was hard. They raised
heavy tributes. Their policy was one of extreme
centralization, and, without destroying the religion of
the peoples conquered by their arms, they imposed
upon them the worship and the supremacy of their
own national deities. Their warlike expeditions bore
a pronounced religious character. The priests marched
at the head of the soldiers, and bore Aztec idols on
their backs. On the eve of a battle they kindled fresh
fire by the friction of wood; and it was they who gave

the signal of attack. These wars had pillage and conquest as their object, but also and very specially the
capture of victims to sacrifice to the Aztec gods. For
the Aztecs pushed the superstitious practice of human
sacrifice to absolute frenzy. It was to these horrible
sacrifices that they attributed their successes in war
and the prosperity of their empire. If they experienced
a check or had suffered any disaster, they redoubled
their blood-stained offerings. But note this trait, so
essentially pagan and in such perfect accord with the
polytheistic ideas of the ancient world—they sacrificed
to the gods of the conquered country too, to show
them that it was not against them they were contend-
ing, and that the new régime would not rob them of
the homage to which they were accustomed. The
Aztec deities were not *jealous.* They confined themselves to vindicating their own pre-eminence. After
each fresh conquest, the Aztecs raised a temple at
Mexico bearing the name of the conquered country,
and thither they transported natives of the place to
carry on the worship after their own customs. It
seems that they did not consider even this precaution
enough; for they constructed a special edifice near the
great temple of Mexico, where the supreme deities of
the Aztec people were enthroned, and there they shut
up the idols of the conquered countries. This was to
prevent their escape, should the desire come over them

to return to their own peoples and help them to revolt.[1]

All this will explain how it was that Fernando Cortes found numerous allies against Montezuma's despotism amongst the native peoples. For it is an error, generally received indeed, but contradicted by history, that the Spanish captain decided the fate of so redoubtable an empire, and of a city so vigorously defended as Mexico, with the sole aid of his thousand Europeans.

For the rest, we are forced to acknowledge that the Aztecs had developed their civilization, in its political and material aspects, in a way that does the greatest credit to their sagacity. Property was organized on the individual and hereditary basis for the noble families, and on the collective basis for the people, divided into communities. The taxes were raised in kind, according to fixed rules. Numbers of slaves were charged with the most laborious kinds of work. The merchants, assembled in the cities, formed a veritable *tiers-état* which exercised a growing political influence. There were markets, the abundance and wealth of which stupefied the Spaniards. The luxury of the court and of the great families was dazzling. No one dared to address the sovereign save with lowered

---

[1] See *Sahagun*, Tom. I. p. 201, Appendix to Lib. ii. (Vol. II. p. 174, in Jourdanet's translation).

voice, and—strange custom in our eyes!—no one appeared before him save with naked feet and clad in sordid garments, in sign of humility. Mexico had been joined to the mainland by causeways, along which an aqueduct conveyed the pure waters of distant springs to the city. The irrigation works in the country were numerous and in good repair. The streets were cleansed by day and lighted at night, advantages in which none of the European capitals rejoiced in the sixteenth century. And finally, for we cannot dwell indefinitely upon this subject, let us note the excellent roads that stretched from Mexico to the limits of the Aztec empire and the confederated states. Along these roads the sovereigns of Mexico had established, at intervals of two leagues, courier posts for the transmission of important news to them. Montezuma heard of the disembarkment of Fernando Cortes three days after it took place.

And now imagine that this people was always averse to navigation—was ignorant of use of iron, knowing only of gold, silver and copper—had no beast of traction or burden, neither horse, nor ass, nor camel, nor elephant, nor even the llama of Peru—was without writing (for though we find a kind of hieroglyph on the monuments of Mexico and Central America, yet the system was not of the smallest avail for ordinary life)—and, finally, had no money except an inconsiderable number of silver crosses and cacao berries, the mass of exchanges being effected by barter! On the other hand, they worked in stone with admirable skill. In their knives and lance and arrow heads, made of obsidian, they achieved remarkable perfection, and they excelled in the art of supplying the place of writing by pictures, painted on a kind of aloe paper or on cotton stuffs, representing the persons or things as to which they desired to convey information.

Such, then, is the singular people that Spain was destined to conquer in the sixteenth century, and whose civilization, though modified by the special Aztec spirit, rested after all upon the same bases that had sustained the more ancient civilization of Central America. And this is equally true of the religion, which, with all the varieties impressed upon it by the special genius or inclinations of the diverse peoples, reveals itself as resting upon one common basis, from the Isthmus of Panama to the Gulf of California and the mouths of the Rio del Norte.

IV.

One of the fundamental traits of this regional religion, then, is the pre-eminence of the Sun, regarded as a personal and animated being, over all other divinities. At Guatemala, amongst the Lacandones, he was adored

directly, without any images. Amongst their neighbours the Itzas, not far from Vera Paz, he was represented as a round human head encircled by diverging
rays and with a great open mouth. This symbol,
indeed, was very widely spread in all that region. Often
the Sun is represented putting out his tongue, which
means that he lives and speaks. For in the American
hieroglyphics, a protruded tongue, or a tongue placed
by the side of any object, is the emblem of life. A
mountain with a tongue represents a volcano. The
Sun was generally associated with the Moon as spouse,
and they were called *Grandfather* and *Grandmother.*
In Central America, and in the territory of Mexico,
may be observed a number of stone columns which
are likewise statues ; but the head is generally in the
middle, and is so overlaid with ornaments or attributes,
that it is not very easy to discover it. These are *Sun-
columns.* As he traced the shadow of these monoliths upon the soil day after day, the Sun appeared to
be caressing them, loving them, taking them as his
fellow-workers in measuring the time. These same
columns were also symbols of fructifying power.
Often the Sun has a child, who is no other than a
doublet of himself, but conceived in human form as
the civilizer, legislator and conqueror, bearing diverse
names according to the peoples whose hero-god and
first king he is represented as being. And for that

matter, if we had but the time, we might long dwell on the myths of Yucatan, of Guatemala (amongst the Quichés), of Honduras, and of Nicaragua. By the side of the Sun and Moon, grandfather and grandmother, there were a number of great and small deities (some of them extremely vicious), and amongst others a god of rain, who was called Tohil by the Quichés and Tlaloc at Mexico, where he took his place amongst the most revered deities. His name signifies " noise," " rumbling." Amongst the Quichés he had a great temple at Utatlan, pyramidal in form, like all others in this region of the world, where he was the object of a " perpetual adoration " offered him by groups of from thirteen to eighteen worshippers, who relieved each other in relays day and night.

Human sacrifice was practised by all these peoples, though not to such an extent as amongst the Aztecs, for they only resorted to it on rare occasions. It was especially girls that they immolated, with the idea of giving brides to the gods. They were to exercise their conjugal influence in favourably disposing their divine consorts towards the sacrificers. In this con- nection we find a tragi-comic story of a young victim whose forced marriage was not in the least to her taste, and who threatened to pronounce the most terrible maledictions from heaven upon her slaughterers. Her threats had so much effect that they let her go, and procured another and less recalcitrant bride for the deity.[1]

Finally, we will mention a most characteristic deity (whom we shall presently recognize at Mexico under yet another name), variously known as Cuculkan (bird-serpent), Gucumatz (feathered-serpent), Hurakan —whence our " hurricane "—Votan (serpent), &c. He is always a serpent, and generally feathered or flying. He is a personification of the wind, especially of the east wind, which brings the fertilizing rains in that district. Almost everywhere he is credited with gentle and beneficent dispositions, and therefore with a certain hostility to human sacrifice. It was this deity, in one of his forms, who was worshipped in the sacred island of Cozumel, situated close to Yucatan, to which pilgrimages were made from great distances. It was there that the Spaniards, to their great surprise, first observed a cross surmounting the temple of this god of the wind. This was the starting-point of the legend according to which the Apostle Thomas had of old evangelized America. It is a pure illusion. The pagan cross of Central America and Mexico is nothing whatever but the symbol of the four cardinal points of the compass from which blow the four chief winds.

Such is the common religious basis, which we have

[1] The story is given by *Bancroft*, Vol. III. p. 471, on the authority of *Lopez Medel*.

simply sketched in its most general outlines, and upon which the more elaborate and sombre religion of the Aztecs, which we shall examine at our next meeting, was reared. Pray observe that we find in this group of connected beliefs and worships something quite analogous to the polytheism of the ancient world. The only notable difference is, that the god of Heaven, Dyaus, Varuna, Zeus, Ahura Mazda, or (in China) Tien, does not occupy the same pre-eminent place in the American mythology that he takes in its European and Asiatic counterparts. For the rest, the processes of the human spirit are absolutely identical in the two continents. In both alike it is the phenomena of nature, regarded as animated and conscious, that wake and stimulate the religious sentiment and become the objects of the adoration of man. At the same time, and in virtue of the same process of internal logic, these personified beings come to be regarded more and more as possessed of a·nature superior in power indeed, but in all other respects closely conforming, to that of man. If nature-worship, with the animism that it engenders, shapes the first law to which nascent religion submits in the human race, anthropomorphism furnishes the second, disengaging itself ever more and more completely from the zoomorphism which gener-ally serves as an intermediary. This is so *everywhere*. And thus we may safely leave to ethnologists the task of deciding whether the whole human race descends from one original couple or from many; for, spiritually speaking, humanity in any case is one. It is one same spirit that animates it and is developed in it; and this, the incontestable unity of our race, is likewise the only unity we need care to insist on. Let us recognize it, then, since indeed it imposes itself upon us, and let us confess that the gospel did but anticipate the last word of science in proclaiming universal fraternity.

And here, Gentlemen, we reach one of those grand generalizations which must finally win over even those who are still inclined to distrust the philosophical history of religions as a study that destroys the most precious possessions of humanity. In setting forth the intellectual and moral unity of mankind, everywhere directed by the same successive evolutions and the same spiritual laws, it brings into light the great principal of *human brotherhood*. In demonstrating that these evolutions, in spite of all the influences of ignorance, of selfishness and of grossness, converge towards a sublime, ideal goal, and are no other than the mysterious but mighty and unbroken attraction to that unfathomable Power of which the universe is the visible expression, it founds on a basis of reason the august sentiment of the *divine fatherhood*. Brothermen and one Father-God!—what more does the thinker need to raise the dignity of our nature, the promises of the future, the sublimity of our destiny, into a region where the inconstant waves of a superficial criticism can never reach them? Such is the vestibule of the eternal Temple; and in approaching the sanctuary—albeit I may not know the very title by which best to call the Deity who reigns in it—I bow my head with that union of humility and of filial trust which constitutes the pure essence of religion.

But from these general considerations we must return to our more immediate subject. At our next meeting, Gentlemen, we are to study the special beliefs and mythology of ancient Mexico.

LECTURE II.

THE DEITIES AND MYTHS OF MEXICO.

II

THE DEITIES AND MYTHS OF MEXICO.

It will be my task to-day to give an account of the Mexican mythology and religion, resting as it does on the foundation common to the peoples of Central America, but inspired by the sombre, utilitarian, matter-of-fact, yet vigorous and earnest, genius of the Aztecs. You will remember that this name belongs to the warlike and commercial people that enjoyed, at the beginning of the sixteenth century, a military and political supremacy in the region that is now called Mexico, after the Aztec capital of that name.

I.

To begin with, we must note that the ancient Central-American cultus of the Sun and Moon, considered as the two supreme deities, was by no means renounced by the Aztecs, Ometecutli (i.e. *twice Lord*) and Omecihuatl (*twice Lady*), or in other words supreme Lord and Lady, are the designations under which they are always indicated in the first rank in the religious for-

mulæ. All the Mexicans called themselves "children
of the Sun," and greeted him every morning with
hymns and with trumpet peals, accompanied with
offerings. Four times by day and four times by night,
priests who were attached to the various temples
addressed their devotions to him. And yet he had no
temple specially consecrated to him. The fact was that
all temples were really his, much as in our own Christian civilization all the churches are raised in honour
of God, though particular designations are severally
given to them. The Sun was the *teotl* (i. e. the god) *par
excellence*. I am informed that to this very day the inhabitants of secluded parts of Mexico, as they go to mass,
throw a kiss to the sun before entering the church.

Notwithstanding all this, we have to observe that,
by an inconsistency which again has its analogies in
other religions, the cultus of the supreme deity and
his consort was pretty much effaced in the popular
devotions and practices by that of divinities who were
perhaps less august, and in some cases were even
derived from the substance of the supreme deity
himself, but in any case seemed to stand nearer to
humanity than he did. More especially, the national
deities of the Aztecs, the guardians of their empire,
whose worship they instituted wherever their arms had
triumphed, practically took the first place. It is with
these national deities that we are now to make acquaint-

ance, and we cannot do better than begin with the two great deities of the city of Mexico, whose colossal statues were enthroned on its principal temple.

But first we must form some notion of what a Mexican temple was.

The word "temple," if held to imply an enclosed and covered building, is very improperly applied to the kind of edifice in question. Indeed, a Mexican temple (and the same may be said of most of the sanctuaries of Central America) was essentially a gigantic altar, of pyramidal form, built in several stages, contracting as they approached the summit. The number of these retreating stories or terraces might vary. There were never less than three, but there might be as many as five or six, and in Tezcuco some of these quasi-pyramids even numbered nine. The one that towered over all the rest in the city of Mexico was built in five stages. It measured, at its base, about three hundred and seventy-five feet in length and three hundred in width, and was over eighty feet high. At a certain point in each terrace was the stair that sloped across the side of the pyramid to the terrace above; but the successive ascents were so arranged that it was necessary to make the complete circuit of the edifice in order to mount from one stage to another, and consequently the grand processions to which the Mexicans were so much devoted must have encircled the whole edifice from top to bottom, like a huge living serpent, before the van could reach the broad platform at the top, and this must have added not a little to the picturesque effect of these religious ceremonies. Such an erection was called a *teocalli* or "abode of the gods." The great teocalli of Mexico commanded the four chief roads that parted from its base to unite the capital to all the countries beneath the sceptre of its rulers. It was the palladium of the empire, and, as at Jerusalem, it was the last refuge of the defenders of the national independence.

The teocalli which Fernando Cortes and his companions saw at Mexico, and which the conqueror razed to the ground, to replace it by a Catholic church, was not of any great antiquity. It had been constructed thirty-four years before, in the place of another much smaller one that dated from the time when the Aztecs were but an insignificant tribe; and it seems that frightful human hecatombs had ensanguined the foundations of this, more recent teocalli. Some authorities speak of seventy-two or eighty thousand victims, while more moderate calculations reduce the number to twenty thousand, which is surely terrible enough. In front of the temple there stretched a spacious court some twelve hundred feet square. All around were smaller buildings, which served as habitations for the priests, and store-houses for the apparatus of worship, as well as arsenals, oratories for the sovereign and the grandees of the empire, chapels for the inferior deities and so on. Amongst these buildings was the temple in which, as I have said, the gods of the conquered peoples were literally imprisoned. In another the Spaniards could count a hundred and thirty-six thousand symmetrically-piled skulls. They were the skulls of all the victims that had been sacrificed since the foundation of the sanctuary. And, by a contrast no less than monstrous, side by side with this monument of the most atrocious barbarism there were halls devoted to the care of the poor and sick, who were tended gratuitously by priests.[1] What a tissue of contradictions is man!

But the Aztec religion does not allow us to dwell upon the note of tenderness. In the centre of the broad platform at the summit stood the *stone of sacrifices*, a monolith about three feet high, slightly ridged on the surface. Upon this stone the victim was . stretched supine, and while sundry subordinate priests held his head, arms and feet, the sacrificing pontiff raised a heavy knife, laid open his bosom with one terrific blow, and tore out his heart to offer it all bleeding and palpitating to the deity in whose honour the sacrifice was performed. And here you will recog-

---

[1] See *Torquemada*, Lib. viii. cap. xx. at the end. On the Mexican temples in general, see *Müller*, pp. 644–646.

nize that idea, so widely spread in the two Americas, and indeed almost everywhere amongst uncivilized peoples, that the heart is the epitome, so to speak, of the individual—his soul in some sense—so that to appropriate his heart is to appropriate his whole being.

Finally, there rose on the same platform a kind of chapel in which were enthroned the two chief deities of the Aztecs, Uitzilopochtli and Tezcatlipoca.[1] And here I will ask you to accompany Captain Bernal Diaz in the retinue of his chief, Fernando Cortes, to whom the king Montezuma himself had seen fit to do the honours of his "cathedral." For, as you are aware, Montezuma, divided between a rash confidence and certain apprehensions which I shall presently explain, received Cortes for a considerable time with the utmost distinction, lodged him in one of his palaces, and did everything in the world to please him. This, then, is the narrative of Bernal Diaz:[2]

"Montezuma invited us to enter a little tower, where in a kind of chamber, or hall, stood what appeared like two altars covered with rich embroidery." (What Bernal Diaz compared

[1] On the great temple of Mexico and its annexes, see *Waitz*, IV. 148 sqq., where the scattered data of Sahagun, Acosta, Gomara, Bernal Diaz, Ixtlilxochitl, Clavigero, &c., are drawn together. See also *Bancroft*, II. 577—587, III. 430 sq.

[2] Op. cit. cap. xcii.

to altars were the two *Teoicpalli* (or *seats of the gods*), which were wooden pedestals, painted azure blue and bearing a serpent's head at each corner). . . . . " The first [idol], placed on the right, we were told represented Huichilobos, their god of war" (this was as near as Bernal Diaz could get to Uitzilopochtli), "with his face and countenance very broad, his eyes monstrous and terrible; all his body was covered with jewels, gold and pearls of various sizes. . . . . His body was girt with things like great serpents, made with gold and precious stones, and in one hand he held a bow, and arrows in the other. And another little idol who stood by him, and, as they said, was his page, carried a short lance for him, and a very rich shield of gold and jewels. And Huichilobos had his neck hung round with faces of Indians, and what seemed to be the hearts of these same Indians, made of gold, or some of them of silver, covered with blue gems; and there stood some brasiers there, containing incense made with copal and the hearts of three Indians who had been slain that same day; and they were burning, and with the smoke and incense they had made that sacrifice to him; and all the walls of this oratory were so bathed and blackened with cakes of blood, as was the very ground itself, that the whole exhaled a very foul odour.

" Carrying our eyes to the left we perceived another great mass, as high as Huichilobos. Its face was like a bear's, and its shining eyes were made of mirrors called *Tezcat*. Its body was covered with rich gems like that of Huichilobos, for they said that they were brothers. And this Tescatepuca" (the mutilated form under which Bernal Diaz presents Tezcatlipoca) "was the god of hell" (this is another mistake, for Tezcatlipoca was a celestial deity). . . . " His body was surrounded with figures like little imps, with tails like serpents;

and the walls were so caked and the ground so saturated with blood, that the slaughter-houses of Castile do not exhale such a stench ; and indeed we saw the hearts of five victims who had been slaughtered that same day. . . . . And since everything smelt of the shambles, we were impatient to escape from the foul odour and yet fouler sight."

II.

Such was the impression made upon a Spanish soldier and a good Catholic by the sight of the two chief deities of the Mexican people. To him they were simply two abominable inventions of Satan. Let us try to go a little further below the surface.

Uitzilopochtli signifies *Humming-bird to the left,* from *Uizilin* (Humming-bird), and *opochtli* (to the left). The latter part of the name is probably due to the position we have just seen noticed to the left of the other great deity, Tezcatlipoca. But why Humming-bird ? What can there be in common between this graceful little creature and the monstrous idol of the Aztecs ? The answer is given by the American mythology, in which the Humming-bird is a divine being, the messenger of the Sun. In the Aztec language it is often called the " sun-beam " or the " sun's hair." This charming little bird, with the purple, gold and topaz sheen of its lovely plumage, as it flits amongst the flowers like a butterfly, darts out its long tongue before it to extract their juices, with a burring of its wings like the humming of bees, whence it derives its English name. Moreover, it is extremely courageous, and will engage with far larger birds than itself in defence of its nest. In the northern regions of Mexico, the humming-bird is the messenger of spring, as the swallow is with us. At the beginning of May, after a cold and dry season that has parched the soil and blighted all verdure, the atmosphere becomes pregnant with rain, the sun regains his power, and a marvellous transformation sets in. The land arrays itself, before the very eyes, with verdure and flowers, the air is filled with perfumes, the maize comes to a head, and hosts of humming-birds appear, as if to announce that the fair season has returned. We may lay it down as certain that the humming-bird was the object of a religious cultus amongst the earliest Aztecs, as the divine messenger of the Spring, like the wren amongst our own peasantry, the plover amongst the Latins, and the crow amongst many tribes of the Red skins. It was the emissary of the Sun.

It was in this capacity, and under the law of anthropomorphism to which all the Mexican deities were subject, that the divine humming-bird, as a revealing god, the protector of the Aztec nation, took the human form more and more completely in the religious consciousness of his worshippers. And indeed the Mexican mythology gives form to this idea that the divine humming-bird (of which those on earth were but the relatives or little brothers) was a celestial man like an Aztec of the first rank, in the following legend of his incarnation.

Near to Coatepec, that is to say the Mountain of Serpents,[1] lived the pious widow *Coatlicue* or *Coatlantona* (the ultimate meaning of which is "female serpent"). One day, as she was going to the temple to worship the Sun, she saw a little tuft of brilliantly colored feathers fall at her feet. She picked it up and placed it in her bosom to present as an offering to the Sun. But when she was about to draw it forth, she knew not what had come upon her. Soon afterwards she perceived that she was about to become a mother. Her children were so enraged that they determined to kill her, but a voice from her womb cried out to her, "Mother, have no fear, for I will save thee, to thy great honour and my own great glory." And in fact Coatlicue's children failed in their murderous attempt. In due time Uitzilopochtli was born, grasping his shield and lance, with a plume of feathers shaped like a bird's beak on his head, with humming-birds' feathers on his left leg, and his face, arms and legs barred with blue. Endowed from his birth with extraordinary strength, while still an infant he put to death those

[1] Compare the German "Schlangenberg" and the old French "Guivremont."

who had attempted to slay his mother, together with all who had taken their part. He gave her everything he could take from them; and after accomplishing mighty feats on behalf of the Aztecs, whom he had taken under his protection, he re-ascended to heaven, bearing his mother with him, and making her henceforth the goddess of flowers.[1]

You will be struck by the analogy between this myth and more than one Greek counterpart. There is the same method of reducing to the conditions of human life, and concentrating at a single point of time and space, a permanent or regularly recurrent and periodic natural phenomenon. Titzilopochtli, the humming-bird, has come from the Sun with the purpose of making himself man, and he has therefore taken flesh in an Aztec woman, Coatlicue, the serpent, who is no other than the spring florescence, and therefore the Mexican Flora. It is not only amongst the Mexicans that the creeping progress of the spring vegetation, stretching along the ground towards the North, has suggested the idea of a divine serpent crawling over the earth. The Athenian myth of Erichthonius is a conception of the same order. The celestial humming-bird, then, offspring of the Sun, valiant and warlike from the day of his birth, champion of his mother, plundering and ever victorious, is the

[1] See the legend in *Clavigero*, Lib. vi. § 6.

symbol instinctively seized on by the Aztec people:
for it, too, had sprung from humble beginnings, had
been despised and menaced by its neighbours, and had
grown so marvellously in power and in wealth as to
have become the invincible lord of Anahuac. Uitzilopochtli had grown with the Aztec people. He bears,
amongst other surnames, that of Mextli, the warrior,
whence the name of Mexico. He protects his people
and ever extends the boundaries of its empire. And
thus, in spite of his bearing the name of a little bird,
his statue as an incarnate deity had become colossal.
Yet the Aztecs did not lose the memory of his original
minuteness of stature. Did you observe, in the account
given By Bernal Diaz, that there stood at the feet of
the huge idol another quite small one, that served,
according to the Spanish Captain, as his page? This
was the *Uitziton*, or " little humming-bird," called also
the *Paynalton*, or the " little quick one," whose image
was borne by a priest at the head of the soldiers as
they charged the enemy. On the day of his festival,
too, he was borne at full speed along the streets
of the city. He was, therefore, the diminutive
Uitzilopochtli, or more correctly speaking, the Uitzilopochtli of the early days, the portable idol of
the still wandering tribe; and in fidelity to those
memories, as well as to preserve the warlike rite to
the efficacy of which they attached so much value,

the Aztecs had kept the small statue by the side of the great one.

To sum up: Uitzilopochtli was a derivative form or determination of the Sun, and specifically of the Sun of the fair season. He had three great annual festivals. The first fell in May, at the moment of the return of the flowering vegetation. The second was celebrated in August, when the favourable season unfolded all its beauty. The third coincided with our month of December. It was the beginning of the cold and dry season. On the day of this third festival they made a statue in Uitzilopochtli's likeness, out of dough concocted with the blood of sacrificed infants, and, after all kinds of ceremonies, a priest pierced the statue with an arrow. Uitzilopochtli would die with the verdure, the flowers and all the beauteous adornments of spring and summer. But, like Adonis, like Osiris, like Atys, and so many other solar deities, he only died to live and to return again.[1]

It was now his brother Tezcatlipoca who took the direction of the world. His name signifies "Shining Mirror." As the Sun of the cold and sterile season, he turned his impassive glance upon all the world, or gazed into the mirror of polished crystal that he held in his hand, in which all the actions of men were

---

[1] See *Müller,* pp. 602 sqq., and *Sahagun*, Tom. I. pp. 1, 237, sqq., Lib. i. cap. i., and Lib. iii. cap. i., &c.

reflected. He was a stern god of judgment, with whose being ideas of moral retribution were associated. He was therefore much dreaded. Up to a certain point he reminds us of the Vedic Varuna. His statue was made of dark obsidian rock, and his face recalled that of the bear or tapir. Suspended to his hair, which was plaited into a tail and enclosed in a golden net, there hung an ear, which was likewise made of gold, towards which there mounted flocks of smoke in the form of tongues. These were the prayers and supplications of mortals. Maladies, famines and death, were the manifestations of Tezcatlipoca's justice. Dry as the season over which he presided, he was not easily moved. And yet he was not absolutely inexorable. The ardent prayers, the sacrifices and the supplications of his priests might avert the strokes of his wrath. But in spite of all, he was pre-eminently the god of austere law. And this is why he was regarded as the civilizing and organizing deity of the Aztecs. It was he who had established the laws that governed the people and who watched over their observance. In this capacity he made frequent journeys of inspection, like an invisible prefect of police, through the city of Mexico, to see what was going on there. Stone seats had been erected in the streets for him to rest upon on these occasions, and no mortal would have dared to occupy them. At the same time

a terrible and cruel subtlety in the means he employed
to accomplish his ends was attributed to him ; and the
legend about him, which is far less brilliant than that
of his brother Uitzilopochtli, led several Europeans to
believe that he was simply an ancient magician who
had spread terror around him by his sorceries. All
this we see exemplified in his conflicts with a third
great deity whom we shall next describe. In any case
we may define Tezcatlipoca as another determination
of the Sun, and specifically of the winter Sun of the
cold, dry, sterile season.[1]

The third great deity is Quetzalcoatl, that is to say
"the feathered serpent," or " the serpent-bird ;" and
it is specially noteworthy, in connection with the elevated rank which he occupied in the Mexican pantheon,
that he was not an Aztec deity, but one of the ancient
gods of the invaded country. He was in fact a Toltec
deity, and we recognize in his name, as well as in the
special notes in the legend concerning him, that god
of the wind whom we know already in Central America
under the varying names of Cuculcan, Hurakan, Gucumatz, Votan and so forth. He is almost always a
serpent, and a serpent with feathers. His temple at

---

[1] See *Clavigero*, Lib. vi. ₰ 2. *Acosta*, pp. 324 sqq., Lib. v. cap. ix.
(pp. 353 sq. in E. G.'s translation); *Sahagun*, Tom. I. pp. 2 sq., 241
sq., Lib. i. cap. iii., Lib. iii. cap. ii. See also *Ternaux-Compans*, Vol.
XII. p. 18.

Mexico departed altogether from the pyramidal type that we have described. It was dome-shaped and covered. The entrance was formed by a great serpent-mouth, wide open and showing its fangs, so that the Spaniards thought it represented a gate of hell. Quetzalcoatl's priests were clothed in white, whereas the ordinary garb of the Mexican priests was black. There was something mysterious and occult about the priesthood of this deity, as though it were possessed of divine secrets or promises, the importance of which it would be dangerous to undervalue. A special aversion to human sacrifice, and especially to the frightful abuse of the practice amongst the Aztecs, was attributed to this god and his priests, in passive protest, as it were, against the sanguinary rites to which the Aztecs attributed the prosperity of their empire.

` The legend of Quetzalcoatl, as the Aztecs transmitted it to the Spaniards, is a motley concatenation of euhemerized myths. Its historical basis is the continuous retreat of the Toltecs before the northern invaders, with their god Tezcatlipoca. This latter deity becomes a magician, cunning and malicious enough to get the better of the gentle Quetzalcoatl on every occasion. I regret that time will not allow me to tell in detail of the combat between Tezcatlipoca and Quetzalcoatl. The latter was a sovereign who lived long ago at Tulla, the northern focus of Toltec civilization. Under his sceptre men lived in great happiness and enjoyed abundance of everything. He had taught them agriculture, the use of the metals, the art of cutting stone, the means of fixing the calendar; and being opposed to the sacrifice of human victims —note this—he had advised their replacement by the drawing of blood from the tongue, the lips, the chest, the legs, &c. Tezcatlipoca succeeded by his enchantments in destroying this rule of peace and prosperity, and forced Quetzalcoatl to quit Tulla, which thereupon fell in ruins. He then pursued him into Cholula, the ancient sacred city of the Toltecs, in which he had sought refuge, and in which he had again made happiness and abundance reign. Finally, he forced him to quit the continent altogether, and embark in a mysterious vessel not far from Vera Cruz, near to the very spot where Cortes disembarked. Since then Quetzalcoatl had disappeared; "But wait!" said his priests, "for he will return." This expectation of Quetzalcoatl's return furnishes a kind of parallel to the Messianic hope, or more closely yet to the early Christian expectation of the *parousia* or "second coming" of the Christ. For when he returned, it would be to punish his enemies, to chastise the wicked, the oppressors and the tyrants. And that is why the Aztecs dreaded his return, and why they had not dared to proscribe his cultus, but, on the contrary, recognized it and

carried it on. And if you would know the real secret
of the success of Fernando Cortes in his wild enter-
prise—for, after all, the Mexican sovereign could easily
have crushed him and his handful of men, by making
a hecatomb of them before they had had time to
entrench themselves and make allies— you will find it
in the fact that Montezuma, whose conscience was
oppressed with more crimes than one, had a very lively
dread of Quetzalcoatl's return; and when he was
informed that at the very point where the dreaded god
had embarked, to disappear in the unknown East,
strange and terrible beings had been seen to disembark,
bearing with them fragments of thunderbolts, in tubes
that they could discharge whenever they would—some
of them having two heads and six legs, swifter of foot
than the fleetest men—Montezuma could not doubt
that it was Quetzalcoatl returning, and instead of send-
ing his troops against Cortes, he preferred to negotiate
with him, to allow him to approach, and to receive
him in his own palace. And although doubts soon
asserted themselves in his mind, yet he long retained,
perhaps even to the last, a superstitious dread of Cortes,
that enabled the latter to secure a complete ascendancy
over him. This, I repeat, was the secret of the bold
Spaniard's success; nor can we ever understand the
matter rightly unless we take into consideration the
significance of this worship of Quetzalcoatl that the

Aztecs had continued to respect, though all the while flattering themselves that their own god, Tezcatlipoca, would be able once more to protect them against his ancient adversary. Years after the conquest, Father Sahagun had still to answer the question of the natives, who asked him what he knew of the country of Quetzalcoatl.[1]

What, then, was the fundamental significance of this feathered Serpent that so pre-occupied the religious consciousness of the Aztecs.

He was not the Sun. The Sun does not disappear in the East. He was a god of the wind, as Father Sahagun perfectly well understood, but of that wind in particular that brings over the parched land of Mexico the tepid and fertilizing exhalations of the Atlantic. And this is why Tezcatlipoca, the god of the cold and dry season, rather than Uitzilopochtli, is his personal enemy. It is towards the end of the dry season that the fertilizing showers begin to fall on the eastern shores, and little by little to reach the higher lands of the interior. The flying Serpent, then, the wind that

---

[1] On Quetzalcoatl, see *Müller*, pp. 577—590; *Bancroft*, Vol. III. pp. 239—287; *Torquemada*, Lib. vi. cap. xxiv., Lib. iii. cap. vii.; *Claverigo*, Lib. vi. § 4; *Ixtlilxochitl* in *Ternaux-Compans*, Vol. XII. pp. 5—8 (further, pp. 9—27 of the same volume on the Toltecs); *Prescott*, Bk. i. chap. iii., Bk. iv. chap. v., and elsewhere; *Sahagun*, Tom. I. pp. 3-4, 245-6, 255—259, Lib. i. cap. v., Lib. iii. capp. iv. xii.—xiv.

comes like a huge bird upon the air, bringing life and abundance with it, is a benevolent deity who spreads prosperity wherever he goes. But he does not always breathe over the land, and does not carry his blessed moisture everywhere. Tezcatlipoca appears. The lofty plateaux of Tulla, of Mexico and of Cholula, are the first victims of his desolating force. Quetzalcoatl withdraws ever further and further to the East, and at last disappears in the great ocean.

Such is the natural basis of the myth of Quetzalcoatl, and the justification of my remark that we find in him the pendant of those deities, serpents and birds in one, who were adored in Central America, and who answered, like Quetzalcoatl, to the idea of the Atlantic wind. He was, in truth, the ancient deity that the Nahuas or Mayas of the civilized immigrations brought with them when they settled in Anahuac and still further North. Like all the other gods of these regions, Quetzalcoatl had assumed the human shape more and more completely. We still possess, especially in the Trocadero Museum at Paris, great blocks of stone on which he is represented as a serpent covered with feathers, coiled up and sleeping till the time comes for him to wake. But there are also statues of him in human form, save that his body is surmounted by a bird's head, with the tongue projected. Now in the Mexican hieroglyphic this bird's head, with the tongue put out, is no other than the symbol of the wind. Hence, too, his names of *Tohil* "the hummer" or "the whisperer," *Ehecatl* "the breeze," *Nauihehccatl* "the lord of the four winds," &c. The naturalistic meaning of Quetzalcoatl, then, cannot admit of the smallest doubt.

It is probably to the more gentle and humane religious tendency which was kept alive by the priesthood of this deity, that we must attribute the attempted reform of the king of Tezcuco, Netzalhuatcoyotl (the fasting coyote), who has been called the Mexican Solomon. He was a poet and philosopher as well as king, and had no love either of idolatry or of sanguinary sacrifices. He had a great pyramidal teocalli of nine stages erected in his capital for the worship of the god of heaven, to whom he brought no offerings except flowers and perfumes. He died in 1472, and, as far as we can see, his reformation made no progress. The ever-increasing preponderance of the Aztecs was as unfavourable as possible to this humane and spiritual tendency in religion.[1] Yet one loves to dwell upon the fact, that even in the midst of a religion steeped in blood, a protest was inspired by the sentiment of humanity, linked, as it should always be, with the progress of religious thought.

---

[1] See *Clavigero*, Lib. iv. §§ 4, 15, Lib. vii. § 42; *Humboldt*, pp. 319–20, cf. p. 95; *Prescott*, Bk. i. chap. i. and elsewhere; *Bancroft*, Vol. V. pp. 427—429; *Müller*, pp. 526, sq.

III.

We must now proceed with our review of the Mexican deities, but I must be content with indicating the most important amongst them; for without admitting, with Gomara—who registered many names and epithets belonging to one and the same divinity as indicating so many distinct beings—that their number rose to two thousand, we find that the most moderate estimate of the historians raises them to two hundred and sixty. We shall confine ourselves, then, to the most significant.

The importance of rain in the regions of Mexico, so marked in the myths we have already considered, prepares us to find amongst the great gods the figure of Tlaloc, whose name signifies "the nourisher," and who was the god of rain. He was believed to reside in the mountains, whence he sent the clouds. He was also the god of fecundity. Lightning and thunder were amongst his attributes, and his character was no more amiable than that of the Mexican deities in general. His cultus was extremely cruel. Numbers of children were sacrificed to him. His statues were cut in a greenish white stone of the colour of water. In one hand he held a sceptre, the symbol of lightning; in the other, a thunderbolt. He was a cyclops; that is to say, he had but one eye, which shows that he must be ultimately identified as an ancient personification of the rainy sky, whose one eye is the sun. His huge mouth, garnished with crimson teeth, was always open, to signify his greed and his sanguinary tastes. His wife was *Chalchihuitlicue*, "the lady Chalchihuit," whose name is identical with that of a soft green jade stone that was much valued in Mexico. Her numerous offspring, the Tlalocs, probably represent the clouds. Side by side with the hideous sacrifices of which Tlaloc's festival was the occasion, we may note the grotesque ceremony in which his priests flung themselves pell-mell into a pond, imitating the action and the note of frogs. This is but one of a thousand proofs that in the rites intended to conciliate the nature-gods, it was thought well to reproduce in mimicry the actions of those creatures who were supposed to be their favourites or chosen servants. The frogs were manifestly loved by the god of the waters, and to secure his good graces his priests, as was but natural, transformed themselves into frogs likewise. It was with this cultus especially that the symbol of the Mexican cross was connected, as indicating the four points of the horizon from which the wind might blow.

Centeotl was another great deity, a kind of Mexican Ceres or Demeter. She was the goddess of Agriculture, and very specially of maize. Indeed, her name

signifies "maize-goddess," being derived from *ccntli*
(maizc) and *tcotl* (divine being). Sometimes, however,
inasmuch as this goddess had a son who bore the
same name as herself, Centeotl stands for a male
deity. The female deity is often represented with a
child in her arms, like a Madonna. This child, who
is no other than the maize itself, grows up, becomes
an adult god, and is the masculine Centeotl. The
feminine Centeotl, moreover, bears many other names,
such as *Tonantzin* (our revered mother), *Cihuat-
coatl* (lady serpent), and very often *Toci* or *Tocitzin*
(our grandmother). She was sometimes represented
in the form of a frog, the symbol of the moistened
earth, with a host of mouths or breasts on her body.
She had also a daughter, *Xiloncn*, the young maize-
ear, corresponding to the Persephone or Kore of the
Greeks. Her face was painted yellow, the colour of
the maize. Her character, at least among the Aztecs,
had nothing idyllic about it, and we shall have to
return presently to the frightful sacrifices which were
celebrated in her honour.

Next comes the god of Fire, *Xiuhtecutli* (the Lord
of Fire), a very ancient deity, as we see by one of his
many surnames, *Huehueteotl* (the old god). He is
represented naked, with his chin blackened, with a
head-dress of green feathers, carrying on his back a
kind of serpent with yellow feathers, thus combining

the different fire colours. And inasmuch as he looked across a disk of gold, called "the looking-plate," we may ask whether his primitive significance was not very closely allied to that of Tezcatlipoca, the shining mirror of the cold season. Sacrifice was offered to him daily. In every house the first libation and the first morsel of bread were consecrated to him. And finally, as an instance of the astounding resemblance that is forced upon our attention between the religious development of the Old World and that of the New, only conceive that in Mexico, as in ancient Iran and other countries of Asia and Europe, the fire in every house must be extinguished on a certain day in every year, and the priest of Xiuhtecutli kindled fire anew by friction before the statue of his god. You are aware that this rite, with which so many customs and superstitions are connected, rests on the idea that fire is a divine being, of celestial and pure origin, which is shut up in the wood, and which is contaminated in the long run by contact with men and with human affairs. Hence it follows that in order for it to retain its virtues, to continue to act as a purifier and to spread its blessings amongst men, it must be brought down anew, from time to time, from its divine source.[1]

The Aztecs also had a Venus, a goddess of Love,

[1] *Clavigero*, Lib. vi. §§ 5, 15, 34; *Sahagun*, Tom. I. pp. 16—19, Lib. i. cap. xiii.; *Bancroft*, Vol III. p. 385.

who bore the name of *Tlazolteotl* (the goddess of Sensuality).[1]   At Tlascala she was known by the more elegant name of *Xochiquetzal* (the flowery plume). She lived in heaven, in a beautiful garden, spinning and embroidering, surrounded by dwarfs and buffoons, whom she kept for her amusement.   We hear of a battle of the gods of which she was the object.   Though the wife of Tlaloc, she was loved and carried off by Tezcatlipoca.   This probably gives us the clue to her mythic origin.   She must have been the aquatic vegetation of the marsh lands, possessed by the god of waters, till the sun dries her up and she disappears.   The legend about her is not very edifying.   It was she—to mention only a single feat—who prevailed over the pious hermit Yappan, when he had victoriously resisted all other temptations.   After his fall he was changed into a scorpion ; and that is why the scorpion, full of wrath at the memory of his fall and fleeing the daylight, is so poisonous and lives hidden under stones.[2]

We have still to mention *Mixcoatl*, the cloud serpent, whose name survives to our day as the designation of water-spouts in Mexico, and who was specially worshipped by the still almost savage populations of the secluded mountain districts,—*Omacatl*, " the double

[1] See *Sahagun*, Tom. I. pp. 10—16, Lib. i. cap. xii.

[2] See *Boturini*, " Idea de una nueva historia general de la America Septentrional," &c.: Madrid, 1746, pp. 63—65.

reed," a kind of Momus, the god of good cheer, who may very well be a secondary form of Tlaloc, and who avenged himself, when defrauded of due homage, by interspersing hairs and other disagreeable objects amongst the viands,—*Ixtlilton*, "the brown," a sort of Esculapius, the healing god, whose priest concocted a blackish liquid that passed as an efficacious remedy for every kind of disease,—*Yacatecutli*, "the lord guide," the god of travellers and of commerce, whose ordinary symbol was the stick with a carved handle carried by the Mexicans when on a journey, who was sedulously worshipped by the commercial and middle classes of Mexico, and in connection with whom we may note that every Mexican, when travelling, would be careful to fix his stick in the ground every evening and pay his respectful devotions to it,[1]—and, finally, *Xipe*, "the bald," or "the flayed," the god of gold-smiths, probably another form of Uitzilopochtli (whose festival coincided with his), deriving his name apparently from the polishing process to which gold (no doubt regarded as belonging to the substance of the sun) had to undergo to give it the required brilliance, and to whose hideous cultus we shall have to return in our next Lecture.

I must now be brief, and will only speak further of

---

[1] *Bancroft*, Vol. III. pp. 403—417; *Sahagun*, Tom. I. pp. 22—25, 29—33, Lib. i. capp. xv. xvi. xix.

E

the *Tepitoton*, that is to say, the "little tiny ones," minute domestic idols, the number of which was incalculable.   They insensibly lower to the level of animism and fetishism that religion which, as we have seen, bears comparison in its grander aspects with the most renowned mythologies of the ancient world.   I must, however, allow myself a few words on the god *Mictlan*, the Mexican Hades or Pluto.   His name properly signifies "region of the North;" but inasmuch as the North was regarded as the country of mist, of barrenness and of death, his name easily passed into the designation of the subterranean country of the dead. The Germanic *Helle* has a similar history, for it was first localized in the wintry North and then carried underground.   Mictlan, like Hades, was used as a name alike for the sojourn and for the god of the dead. This deity had a consort who bore divers names, and he also had at his command a number of genii or servants, called *Tzitzimitles*, a sort of malicious demons held in great dread by the living.   Of course both Mictlan and his wives are always represented under a hideous aspect, with huge open mouths, or rather jaws, often in the act of devouring an infant.[1]

At last we have done!   In the next Lecture we shall penetrate to the very heart of this singular religion, as we discuss its terrible sacrifices, its institutions,

[1] *Bancroft*, Vol. III. pp. 396—402; *Clavigero*, Lib. vi. §§ 1, 5.

and its doctrines concerning this world and the life to come. And here, again, we shall find cause for amazement in the striking analogies it presents to the rites and institutions of other religions much nearer home. Meanwhile, observe that in examining the purely mythological portion of the subject which we have passed in review to-day, we have seen that there is not a single law manifested by the mythologies of the ancient world, which had not its parallel manifestations in Mexico before it was discovered by the Europeans. The great gods, derived from a dramatized nature—animism, with the fetishism that springs from it, occupying the basement, if I so may express myself, beneath these mythological conceptions—in the midst of all a tendency manifested from time to time towards a purer and more spiritual conception of the adorable Being—all re-appears and all is combined in Mexico, even down to something like an incarnation, and the hope of the coming of the god of justice and of goodness who will restore all things. Indeed, I know not where else one could look for so complete a résumé of what has constituted in all places, now the smallness and wretchedness, now the grandeur and nobleness, of that incomprehensible and irresistible factor of human nature which we call *religion.* The " eternally religious " element in man had stamped its mark upon the unknown Mexico as upon all other lands ; and when at last it was discovered, evidence might have been found, had men been able to appreciate it, that there, too, however frightfully misinterpreted, the Divine breath had been felt.

It is the spiritually-minded who must learn the art of discerning the spirit wherever it reveals itself; and when the horrors rise up before us of which religion has more than once in the course of history been the cause or the pretext, and we are almost tempted to ask whether this attribute of human nature has really worked more good than ill in the destinies of our race, we may remember that the same question might be asked of all the proudest attributes of our humanity. Take polity or the art of governing human societies. To what monstrous aberrations has it not given birth! Take science. Through what lamentable and woful errors has it not pursued its way! Take art. How gross were its beginnings, and how often has it served, not to elevate man, but to stimulate his vilest and most degrading passions! Yet, who would wish to live without government, science or art?

Let us apply the same test to religion. The horrors it has caused cannot weigh against the final and over-mastering good which it produces; and its annals, too often written in blood, should teach us how to guide it, how to purify it from all that corrupts and debases it. We shall see at the close of our Lectures what that directing, normalizing, purifying principle is that must hold the helm of religion and guide it in its evolution. Meanwhile, let no imperfection, no repulsiveness—nay, no atrocity even—blind us to the ideal value of what we have been considering, any more than we should allow the disasters that spring from the use of fire to make us cease to rank it amongst the great blessings of our earthly life.

LECTURE III.

THE SACRIFICES, SACERDOTAL AND MON-
ASTIC INSTITUTIONS, ESCHATOLOGY
AND COSMOGONY OF MEXICO.

III.

THE SACRIFICES, SACERDOTAL AND MON-
ASTIC INSTITUTIONS, ESCHATOLOGY
AND COSMOGONY OF MEXICO.

In our last Lecture we passed in review the chief gods and goddesses of ancient Mexico, and you might see how, in spite of very characteristic differences, the Mexican mythology obeys the same law of formation that manifests itself among the peoples of the Old World, thereby proving once more that the religious development of humanity is not arbitrary, that it proceeds in every case under the direction of the inherent and inalienable principles of the human mind.

To-day we are to complete the internal study of the Mexican religion, by dealing with its sacrifices, its institutions, and its eschatological and cosmogonical doctrines. We begin with those sacrifices of which I have already spoken as so numerous and so horrible.

I.

We have some little difficulty in our times, familiar as we are with spiritual conceptions of God and the divine purposes, in comprehending the extreme importance which sacrifices, offerings, gifts to the divine being, assumed in the eyes of peoples who were still enveloped in the darkness of polytheism and idolatry. And perhaps we may find it more difficult yet to realize the primitive object and intention of these sacrifices. There can be no doubt that they were originally suggested by the idea that the divine being, whatever it may have been—whether a natural object, an animal, or a creature analogous to man— liked what we liked, was pleased with what pleases us, and had the same tastes and the same proclivities as ours. This is the fundamental idea that urged the polytheistic peoples along the path of religious anthropomorphism.

This principle once established, and the object being to secure the good-will and the protection of the divine beings, what could be more natural than to offer them the things in which men themselves took pleasure, such as viands, drinks, perfumes, handsome ornaments, slaves and wives? We must not carry back to the origins of sacrifice the metaphysical and moral ideas which did not really appear until much later. And since the necessity of eating, and the pleasure of eating choice food, take a foremost rank in the estimation of infant peoples, it is not surprising that the food-offering was the most frequent and the most important amongst them, so as in some sort to absorb all the rest.

And here we are compelled to bow before a fact which cannot possibly be disputed, namely, that traces of the primitive sacrifice of human victims meet us everywhere. And this shows that cannibalism, which is now restricted to a few of the savage tribes who have remained closest to the animal life, was once universal to our race. For no one would ever have conceived the idea of offering to the gods a kind of food which excited nothing but disgust and horror amongst men.

This being granted, two rival tendencies must be reckoned with. In the first place, moral development with its influence on religious ideas, worked towards the suppression of the horrible custom of human sacrifice, whilst at the same time extirpating the taste and desire for human flesh. For we must not forget that where cannibalism still reigns, human flesh is regarded as the most delicious of foods; and the Greek mythology has preserved legends and myths that are connected with the very epoch at which human sacrifices first became an object of horror to gods and men. But, in the second place, in virtue of the strange persistency of rights and usages connected with religion, human sacrifices prevailed in many places when cannibalism had completely disappeared from the habits and

tastes of the population.   Thus the Semites of Western
Asia and the Çivaïte Hindus, the Celts, and some of the
populations of Greece and Italy, long after they had
renounced cannibalism, still continued to sacrifice
human beings to their deities.

And this gives us the clue to a third phase, which
was actually realized in Mexico before the conquest.
Cannibalism, in ordinary life, was no longer practised.
The city of Mexico underwent all the horrors of
famine during the siege conducted by Fernando
Cortes.   When the Spaniards finally entered the city,
they found the streets strewn with corpses, which is a
sufficient proof that human flesh was not eaten even
in dire extremities.   And, nevertheless, the Aztecs
not only pushed human sacrifices to a frantic extreme,
but they were *ritual cannibals*, that is to say, there
were certain occasions on which they ate the flesh of
the human victims whom they had immolated.

This practice was connected with another religious
conception, grafted upon the former one.   Almost
everywhere, but especially amongst the Aztecs, we find
the notion that the victim devoted to a deity, and therefore destined to pass into his substance and to become
by assimilation an integral part of him, is already
co-substantial with him, has already become part of
him ; so that the worshipper in his turn, by himself
assimilating a part of the victim's flesh, unites himself

in substance with the divine being. And now observe that in all religions the longing, whether grossly or spiritually apprehended, to enter into the closest possible union with the adored being is fundamental. This longing is inseparable from the religious sentiment itself, and becomes imperious wherever that sentiment is warm; and this consideration is enough to convince us that it is in harmony with the most exalted tendencies of our nature, but may likewise, in times of ignorance, give rise to the most deplorable aberrations.

Note this, again, that immolation or sacrifice cannot be accomplished without suffering to the victim. Yet more: the immense importance of sacrifice in the inferior religions raises the mere rite itself to a position of unrivalled efficacy as gauged by the childlike notions that have given it birth, so that at last it acquires an intrinsic and magical virtue in the eyes of the sacrificers. They have lost all distinct idea as to how their sacrifice gives pleasure to the gods, but they retain the firm belief that as a matter of fact it is the appointed means of acting upon their dispositions and modifying their will. The civilized Greeks and Romans no longer believed that their gods ate the flesh of the sacrifices, but this did not prevent their continuing them as the indispensable means of appeasing the wrath or conciliating the favour of the deities.

To such a length was this carried in India and Iran, that sacrifice finally came to be regarded as a cosmic force, a creative act. The gods themselves sacrificed as a means of creation, or of modifying the existing order of the world. This idea of the intrinsic and magical virtue of sacrifice naturally re-acted on the importance attached to the sufferings of the victim so inseparably connected with it, until the latter came to be regarded as amongst the prime conditions of an efficacious sacrifice. For the rest, I need not do more than mention the notions of substitution of compensation, and of renunciation on the part of the sacrificer, which so readily attach themselves to the idea of sacrifice, and represent its moral aspects.

Now all these considerations will help us to understand both the fearful intensity and the special significance of the practice of human sacrifice established among the Aztecs. And here I must ask you to harden your hearts for a few moments while I conduct you through this veritable chamber of horrors.

The Mexican sacrifices were, in truth, of the most frightful description. It was an axiom amongst the Aztecs that none but human sacrifices were truly efficacious. They were continually making war in order to get a supply of victims. They regarded the victim, when once selected, as a kind of incarnation of the deity who was ultimately to consume his flesh, or at any rate his heart. They retained the practice of cannibalism as a religious rite, and, as though they had some of the Red Skin's blood in their veins, they refined upon the tortures which they forced those victims, whom they had almost adored the moment before, to undergo at last.

These victims were regularly selected, a considererable time in advance. They were vigilantly watched, but in other respects were well cared for and fed with the choicest viands—in a word, fattened. There was not a single festival upon which at least one of these victims was not immolated, and in many cases, great numbers of them were flung upon the " stone of sacrifices," where the priests laid their bosoms open, tore out their hearts, and placed them, as the epitome of the men themselves, in a vessel full of burning rezin or " copal," before the statue of the deity. Some few of these sacrifices it is my duty to describe to you.

For example : To celebrate the close of the annual rule of Tezcatlipoca, which fell at the beginning of May, they set apart a year beforehand the handsomest of the prisoners of war captured during the preceding year. They clothed him in a costume resembling that of the image of the god. He might come and go in freedom, but he was always followed by eight pages, who served at once as an escort and a guard. As he passed, I will not say that the people either knelt or did not kneel before him, for in Mexico the attitude expressive of religious adoration was that of squatting down upon the haunches. As he passed, then, the people squatted all along the streets as soon as they heard the sound of the bells that he carried on his hands and feet. Twenty days before the festival, they redoubled their care and attention. They bathed him, anointed him with perfume, and gave him four beautiful damsels as companions, each one bearing the name of a goddess, and all of them instructed to leave nothing undone to make their divine spouse as happy as possible. He then took part in splendid banquets, surrounded by the great Mexican nobles. But the day before the great festival, they placed him and his four wives on board a royal canoe and carried them to the other side of the lake. In the evening the four goddesses quitted their unhappy god, and his eight guardians conducted him to a lonely *teocalli*, a league distant, where he was flung upon the stone of sacrifices and his heart torn from his bosom. He must disappear and die with the god whom he represented, who must now make way for Uitzilopochtli. This latter deity likewise had his human counterpart, who had to lead a war-dance in his name before being sacrificed. He had the grotesque privilege of choosing the hour of his own immolation, but under the condition that the longer he delayed it the less would his soul be favoured in the abode of Uitzilopochtli. For we must note that in the Mexican order of ideas, though the flesh of the victims was destined to feed the gods to whom they were sacrificed, their souls because the blessed and favoured slaves or servants of these same gods.

Centeotl, or Toci, the goddess of the harvest, had her human sacrifices also, but in this case a woman figured as protagonist. She, too, was dressed like the goddess, and entrusted to the care of four midwives, priestesses of Centeotl, who were commissioned to pet and amuse her. A fortnight before the festival, they celebrated the "arm-dance" before her, in which the dancers, without moving their feet, perpetually raised and lowered their arms, as a symbol of the vegetation fixed at its roots, but moving freely above. Then she had to take part in a mock combat, after which she received the title of "image of the mother of the gods." The day before her execution, she went to pay what was called her "farewell to the market," in which she was conducted to the market of Mexico, sowing maize all along the street as she went, and reverenced by the people as Toci, "our grandmother." But the following midnight she was carried to the top of a teocalli, perched upon the shoulders of a priest, and swiftly decapitated. Then they flayed her without loss of time. The skin of the trunk was chopped off, and a priest, wrapping himself in the bleeding spoil, traversed the streets in procession, and made pretence of fighting with soldiers who were interspersed in the cortége. The skin of the legs was carried to the temple of Centeotl, the son, where another priest made himself a kind of mask with it, to represent his god, and sacrificed four captives in the ordinary way. After this, the priest, accompanied by some soldiers, bore the hideous shreds to a point on the frontier, where they were buried as a talisman to protect the empire.

The festivals of Tlaloc, god of rain, were perhaps yet more horrible. At one of them they sacrificed a number of prisoners of war, one upon another, clothed like the god himself. They tore out their hearts in the usual way, and then carried them in procession, enclosed in a vase, to throw them into a whirlpool of the lake of Mexico, which they imagined to be one of the favoured residences of the aquatic deity. But it was worse still at the festival of this same Tlaloc which fell in February. On this occasion a number of young children were got together, and decked with feathers and precious stones. They put wings upon them, to enable them to fly up, and then placed them on litters, and bore them through the city in grand procession and with the sound of trumpets. The people, says Sahagun,[1] could not choose but weep to see these

---

[1] *Sahagun*, Tom. I. p. 86 (cf. p. 88), Lib. ii. cap. xx.

poor little ones led off to the sacrifice. But if the children themselves cried freely, it was all the better, for it was a sign that the rain would be abundant.[1]

I will not try your nerves by dwelling much longer on this dismal subject, though there is no lack of material. At the feast of Xipe, "the flayed," for example, whole companies of men were wrapped in the skins of sacrificed captives, and engaged in mock battles in that costume. But the only further instance I am compelled to mention is connected with the festival of the god of fire, Xiuhtecutli, which was celebrated with elaborate ceremonies. At set of sun, all who had prisoners of war, or slaves to offer to the deity brought forward their victims, painted with the colours of the god, danced along by their side, and shut them up in a building attached to the teocalli of Fire. Then they mounted guard all round, singing hymns. At midnight, each owner entered and severed a lock of the hair of his slave or slaves, to be carefully preserved as a talisman. At daybreak they brought out the victims and led them to the foot of the temple stair. There the priests took them upon their shoulders and carried them up to the higher platform, where they had prepared a great brazier of burning embers. Here each priest flung his human burden upon the fire, and I leave you to imagine the indescribable scene that en-

[1] *Sahagun* Tom. I. p. 50, Lib. ii. cap i.

sued.   Nor is this all.   The same priests, armed with
long hooks, fished out the poor wretches before they
were quite roasted to death, and despatched them in
the usual fashion on the stone of sacrifices.[1]

It was after these offerings of private devotion that
family and friendly gatherings were held, at which a
part of the victim's flesh was eaten, under the idea that
by thus sharing the food of the deity his worshippers
entered into a closer union with him. We ought,
however, to note that a master never ate the flesh of
his own slave, inasmuch as he had been his guest, and
as it were a member of his family.   He waited till his
friends returned his attention.

II.

Human sacrifice, Gentlemen, appears to have been
a universal practice ; but wherever the human sym-
pathies developed themselves rapidly, it was early
superseded by various substituted rites which it was
supposed might with advantage replace it.   Such were
flagellation, mutilation of some unessential part of the
body, or the emission of a certain quantity of blood.
This last practice, in particular, might be regarded as

---

[1] Compare the detailed description of the festivals of the ancient
religion of Mexico in *Bancroft*, Vol. II. pp. 302—341, Vol. III. pp.
297—300, 330—348, 354—362, 385—396.

an act of individual devotion, a gift made to the gods
by the worshipper himself out of his own very substance. The priesthood of Quetzalcoatl, who had little
taste for human sacrifices, seem to have introduced
this method of propitiating the gods by giving them
one's own blood; and the practice of drawing it from
the tongue, the lips, the nose, the ears or the bosom,
came to be the chief form of expression of individual
piety and penitence in Central America and in Mexico.
The priests in particular owed it to their special character to draw their blood for the benefit of the gods,
and nothing could be stranger than the refined methods
they adopted to accomplish this end. For instance,
they would pass strings or splinters through their lips
or ears and so draw a little blood. But then a fresh
string or a fresh splinter must be added every day, and
so it might go on indefinitely, for the more there were,
the more meritorious was the act; nor can we doubt
that the idea of the suffering endured enhancing the
merit of the deed itself, was already widely spread in
Mexico. There was a system of Mexican *asceticism*,
too, specially characterized by the long fasts which the
faithful, and more particularly the priests, endured.
Indeed, fasting is one of the most general and ancient
forms of adoration. It rests, in the first place, on an
instinctive feeling that a man is more worthy to present
himself before the divine beings when fasting than

when stuffed with food; and, in the second place, on the fact that fasting is shown by experience to promote dreams, hallucinations, extasies and so forth, which have always been considered as so many forms of communication with the deity.[1] It was only later that fasting became the sign and index of mourning, and therefore of sincere repentance and profound sorrow. Mexico had its solitaries or hermits, too, who sought to enter into closer communion with the gods by living in the desert under conditions of the severest asceticism. Are we not once more tempted to exclaim that there is nothing new under the sun?

But the devotees of the ancient Mexican religion had other methods of uniting themselves substantially and corporeally with their gods; and in accordance with the notions which we have seen were accredited by their religion, they had developed a kind (or kinds) of *communion* from which, with a little theology, a regular doctrine of transubstantiation might have been drawn.

Thus, at the third great festival in honour of Uitzilopochtli (celebrated at the time of his death), they

---

[1] Amongst all the indigenous races of North America, prolonged fasting is regarded as the means *par excellence* of securing supernatural inspiration. The Red-skin to become a sorcerer, or to secure a revelation from his *totem*, or the Eskimo to become *Angekok*, will endure the most appalling fasts.

made an image of the deity in dough, steeped it in the blood of sacrificed children, and partook of the pieces.[1] In the same way the priests of Tlaloc kneaded statuettes of their god in dough, cut them up, and gave them to eat to patients suffering from the diseases caused by the cold and wet.[2] The statuettes were first consecrated by a small sacrifice. And so, too, at the yearly festival of the god of fire, Xiuhtecutli, an image of the deity, made of dough, was fixed in the top of a great tree which had been brought into the city from the forest. At a certain moment the tree was thrown down, on which of course the idol broke to pieces, and the worshippers all scrambled for a bit of him to eat.

It has been asked how far any moral idea had penetrated this religion, the repulsive aspects of which we have been describing. The question is a legitimate one. I believe, Gentlemen, that in studying the religious origins of the different peoples of the earth, we shall come to the conclusion that the fusion of the religious and moral life—which has long been an accomplished fact for us, especially since the Gospel, so that we cannot admit the possibility of uniting immorality and piety for a single instant—is not primitive, but

---

[1] *Torquemada*, Lib. vi. cap. xxxviii.; cf. *Sahagun*, Tom. I. p. 174, Lib. ii. cap. xxiv.

[2] *Sahagun*, Tom. I. pp. 35—39, Lib. i. cap. xxi.

is due to the development of the human spirit, and to healthier, more complete and more religious ideas concerning the moral law.   At the beginning of things, and in our own day amongst savages, nay, even amongst the most ignorant strata of the population in civilized countries, it is obvious that religion and morals have extremely little to do with each other.   Some authors, accordingly, in the face of all the monstrous cruelty, selfishness and inhumanity of the Mexican religion, have concluded that no element of morality entered into it at all, but that all was self-seeking and fanaticism.

This is an exaggeration.   We have seen that amongst the nature-gods of Mexico there was one, Tezcatlipoca, who was looked upon as the austere guardian of law and morals.   If we are to believe Father Sahagun,— and even if we allow for strong suspicions as to the accuracy of his translations of the prayers and exhortations uttered under certain circumstances by parents and priests,—it is evident that the Mexicans were taught to consider a decent and virtuous life as required by the gods.   Indeed, they had a system of confession, in which the priest received the statement of the penitent, laid a penance on him, and assured him of the pardon of the gods.   Generally the penitents delayed their confession till they were advanced in age, for relapses were regarded as beyond the reach

of pardon.[1]   It would be nearer the truth to say that
the religious ethics of the Mexicans had entered upon
that path of dualism [2] by which alone, in almost every
case, the normal synthesis or rational reconciliation of
the demands of physical nature and the moral life has
been ultimately reached.   For inasmuch as fidelity to
duty often involves a certain amount of suffering, the
suffering comes to be regarded as the moral act itself,
and artificial sufferings are voluntarily incurred under
the idea that they are the appointed price of access to
a higher and more perfect life, in closer conformity
with the divine will.   The cruel rites which entered
into the very tissue of the Mexican religion could
hardly fail to strengthen the same ascetic tendency, by
encouraging the idea that pain itself was pleasant in
the eyes of the gods.   But the truth is that in this
matter we can discern no more than tendencies.   There
are symptoms of men's minds being busy with the
relation of the moral to the religious life, but no fixed

---

[1] *Sahagun,* Tom. I. pp. 11—16, Tom. II. pp. 57—64, Lib. i. cap
xii., Lib. vi. cap. vii.

[2] Elements were not wanting for the formation of a dualistic system
analagous to Mazdeism.   The *Tzitzimitles* nearly corresponded to the
Iranian *Devas.*   They were a kind of demon servants of Mictlan,
who delighted in springing upon men to devour them, and the protection of the celestial gods was needed to escape from their attacks.
Sahagun, Tom. II. p. 67, Lib. vi. cap viii. (in the middle of a prayer to
Tlaloc).   Cf. also Tom. II. pp. 14 sqq., Lib. v. capp. xi.—xiii.

or systematic conclusions had been reached. It might, perhaps, have been otherwise in the sequel, and these tendencies might ultimately have taken shape in corresponding theories and doctrines, had not the Spanish conquest intervened to put an end forever to the evolution of the Mexican religion.

I have frequently spoken of the Mexican priests, and the time has now come for dwelling more explicitly on this priesthood.

It was very numerous, and had a strong organization reared on an aristocratic basis, into which political calculations manifestly entered. The noblest families (including that of the monarch) had the exclusive privilege of occupying the highest sacerdotal offices. The priests of Uitzilopochtli held the primacy. Their chief was sovereign pontiff, with the title of *Mexicatl-Teo-huatzin*, " Mexican lord of sacred things," and *Teote-cuhtli*, " divine master." Next to him came the chief priest of Quetzalcoatl, who had no authority, however, except over his own order of clergy. He lived as a recluse in his sanctuary, and the sovereign only sent to consult him on certain great occasions ; whereas the primate sat on the privy council and exercised disciplinary powers over all the other priests in the empire. Every temple and every quarter had its regular priests. No one could enter the priesthood until he had passed satisfactorily through certain tests or examinations before the directors of the *Calmecac*, or houses of religious education, of which we shall speak presently. The power of the clergy was very great. They instructed youth, fixed the calendar, preserved the knowledge of the annals and traditions indicated by the hieroglyphics, sang and taught the religious and national hymns, intervened with special ceremonies at birth, marriage and burial, and were richly endowed by taxes raised in kind upon the products of the soil and upon industries. Every successful aspirant to the priesthood, having passed the requisite examinations, received a kind of unction, which communicated the sacred character to him. All this indicates a civilization that had already reached a high point of development; but the indelible stain of the Mexican religion re-appears every moment, even where it seems to rise highest above the primitive religions; amongst the ingredients of the fluid with which the new priest was anointed was the blood of an infant!

The priests' costume in general was black. Their mantles covered their heads and fell down their sides like a veil. They never cut their hair, and the Spaniards saw some of them whose locks descended to their knees. Probably this was a part of the solar symbolism. The rays of the sun are compared to locks of hair, and we very often find the solar heroes or the servants of the Sun letting their hair grow freely in order that they may resemble their god. Their mode of life was austere and sombre. They were subject to the rules of a severe asceticism, slept little, rose at night to chant their canticles, often fasted, often drew their own blood, bathed every night (in imitation of the Sun again), and in many of the sacerdotal fraternities the most rigid celibacy was enforced. You will see, then, that I did not exaggerate when I spoke of the belief that the gods were animated by cruel wills and took pleasure in human pain as having launched the Mexican religion on a path of a systematic dualism and very stern asceticism.[1]

But the surprise we experience in noting all these points of resemblance to the religious institutions of the Old World, perhaps reaches its culminating point when we learn that the Mexican religion actually had its convents. These convents were often, but not always, places of education for both sexes, to which all the free families sent their children from the age of six or nine years upwards. There the boys were taught by monks, and the girls by nuns, the meaning of the hieroglyphics, the way to reckon time, the traditions, the religious chants and the ritual. Bodily exercises

---

[1] On the Mexican priesthood, see *Bancroft*, Vol. II. pp. 200—207, Vol. III. pp. 430—441; *Clavigero*, Lib. vi. §§ 13—17; cf. Lib. iv. § 4; *Humboldt*, pp. 98, 194, 290; *Prescott*, Bk. i. chap. iii.; *Torquemada*, Lib. ix. capp. i.—xxxiv.

likewise had a place in this course of education, which was supposed to be complete when the children had reached the age of fifteen. The majority of them were now sent back to their families, while the rest stayed behind to become priests or simple monks. For there were religious orders, under the patronage of the different gods, and convents for either sex. The monastic rule was often very severe. In many cases it involved abstinence from animal food, and the people called the monks of these severer orders *Quaquacuiltin*, or "herb-eaters." There were likewise asociations resembling our half-secular, half-ecclesiastical fraternities. Thus we hear of the society of the "*Telpochtiliztli*," an association of young people who lived with their families, but met every evening at sunset to dance and sing in honour of Tezcatlipoca. And, finally, we know that ancient Mexico had its hermits and its religious mendicants.[1] The latter, however, only took the vow of mendicancy for a fixed term. These are the details which led von Humboldt and some other writers to believe that Buddhism must have penetrated at some former period into Mexico. Not at all! What we have seen simply proves that asceticism, the war against nature, everywhere clothes itself in similar forms, suggested by the very constitution of man; and there is certainly nothing in common between the gentle insip-

[1] *Camargo* in (Nouv. And. Voy. xcix.,) pp. 134–5.

idity of Buddha's religion and the sanguinary faith of the Aztecs.

The girls were under a rule similar to that of the boys. They led a hard enough life in the convents set apart for them, fasting often, sleeping without taking off their clothes, and (when it was their turn to be on duty) getting up several times in the night to renew the incense that burned perpetually before the gods. They learned to sew, to weave, and to embroider the garments of the idols and the priests. It was they who made the sacred cakes and the dough idols, whose place in the public festivals I have described to you. At the age of fifteen, the same selection took place among the girls as among the boys. Those who stayed in the convent became either priestesses, charged with the lower sacerdotal offices, or directresses of the convents set aside for instruction, or simple nuns, who were known as *Cihuatlamacasque*, "lady deaconesses," or *Cihuaquaquilli*, "lady herb-eaters," inasmuch as they abstained from meat. The most absolute continence was rigorously enforced, and breach of it was punished by death.[1]

[1] *Bancroft*, Vol. II. pp.204—206, Vol. III. pp. 435—436; *Torquemada*, Lib. ix. capp. xiv. xv.; *Sahagun*, Tom. I. pp. 227-8 (last section of Appendix to Lib. ii.); *Acosta*, Lib. v. cap. xvi.; *Clavigero*, Lib. vi. capp. lcvi. xxii.

One cannot but ask whether a priesthood so firmly organized, in which was centred the whole intellectual life and all that can be called the science of Mexico, had not elaborated any higher doctrines or cosmogonic theories such as we owe to the priesthoods of the Old World, especially when we know that they regulated the calendar, which presupposes some astronomical conceptions.

But here we enter upon a region that has not yet been methodically reclaimed by the historians. We have often enough been presented with Mexican cosmogonies, but the fundamental error of all these expositions is, that they present as a fixed and established body of doctrine what was in reality a very loose and unformed mass of traditions and speculations. The sponsors of these cosmogonies agree neither as to their number nor their order of succession, and it is obvious that a mistaken zeal to bring them as near as possible to the Biblical tradition has been at work. An attempt has even been made to find a Mexican Noah, coming out of the ark, in a fish-god emerging from a kind of box floating on the waters.[1]

One thing, however, is certain, namely, that these

[1] See the " Cuadra historico-geroglifico, &c., contributed by Don *José Fernando Ramirez* (curator of the national Museum at Mexico) to *Garcia y Cubas,* "Altas geographico, estadistico e historico de la Republica Mexicana," Entrega 29a (1858).

cosmogonies are not Aztec.   The Aztec deities proper
play no part in them.   We may therefore suppose that
they are of Central American origin, or are due to that
priesthood of Quetzalcoatl which continued its silent
work in the depths of its mysterious retreats.   The
contradictions of our authorities as to the number and
order of these cosmogonies suggest the idea that their
arrangement one after another is no more than a harmonizing attempt to bring various originally distinct
cosmogonies into connection with each other.   The
fact is that others yet are known, in addition to those
which have taken their place in what we may call the
classical list established by Humboldt and Müller.[1]
In this classical list there are five ages of the world,
separated from each other by universal cataclysms,
something after the fashion of the successive creations
of the school of Cuvier.   Each of these ages is called
a Sun, and, according to the elements that preponder-
ate during their respective courses, they are called, 1st,
the Sun of the Earth; 2nd, the Sun of Fire; 3rd, the
Sun of the Air; and 4th, the Sun of Water.   The fifth
Sun, which is the present one, has no special name.
We cannot enter upon the details concerning each of

---

[1] On all that concerns the Mexican cosmogonies, see *Müller*, pp. 477
sq., 509—519; *Bancroft*, Vol. III. pp. 57—65; *Ixtlilxochitl*, "Historia
Chichimeca," capp. i. ii.; *Kingsborough*, "Mexican Antiquities," Vol.
V. pp. 164—167; *Humboldt*, pp. 202—211.

these Suns, and they are not very interesting in any case. They contain confused reminiscences of primitive life, of the ancient populations of Anahuac, of old and bygone worships, but nothing particularly characteristic or original. The only specially striking feature in this mass of cosmogonic traditions is the sense of the instability of the established order alike of nature and society which pervades them. What was it that inspired the Mexicans with this feeling? Perhaps the mighty destructive forces for which tropical countries, equatorial seas and volcanic regions, so often furnish a theatre, had shaken confidence in the permanence of the physical constitution of the world. Perhaps the numerous political and social revolutions, the frequent successions of peoples, rulers and subjects in turn, had accustomed the mind to conceive and anticipate perpetual changes, of which the successive ages of the world were but the supreme expression; and finally, perhaps that quasi-messianic expectation of the return of Quetzalcoatl, to be accompanied by a complete renewal of things, may have given an additional point of attachment to this belief in the caducity of the whole existing order. What is certain is that this sentiment itself was very widely spread. It served as a consolation to the peoples who were crushed beneath the cruel yoke of the Aztecs. They might well cherish the thought that all this would not last for ever;

and even the Aztecs themselves had no unbounded
confidence in the stability of their empire. The Spaniards profited greatly by this vague and all but
universal distrust. After their victory they made much
of pretended prodigies that had shadowed it forth, and
even of prophecies that had announced it.[1] But the
state of mind of the populations concerned being given,
at whatever moment the Spaniards had arrived they
would have been able to appeal to auguries of a like
kind, by dint of just giving them that degree of pre-
cision and clearness which usually distinguishes pre-
dictions that are recorded after their fulfillment!

A further proof that the Mexican religion helped to
spread this sense of the instability of things is furnished
by the grand jubilee festival which was celebrated
every fifty-two years in the city of Mexico and throughout the empire. The Mexican cycle, marking the
coincidence of four times thirteen lunar and four times
thirteen solar years,[2] counted two-and-fifty years, and
was called a " sheaf of years." Now whenever the

---

[1] See *Sahagun*, Tom. II. pp. 281—283, Lib. viii. cap. vi.

[2] The sacerdotal year was lunar. The civil year, which was doubt-
less of later origin, and had been adopted as better suited to the purposes of agriculture, was solar. Every thirteenth year the two coincided. The number *four*, which plays an important part in Mexican
symbolism (cf. the Mexican cross) gave a kind of cosmic significance
to $13 \times 4 = 52$.

dawn of the fifty-third year drew near, the question was anxiously put, whether the world would last any longer, and preparations were made for the great ceremony of the *Toxilmolpilia,* or "binding up of years." The day before, every fire was extinguished. All the priests of the city of Mexico marched in procession to a mountain situated at two leagues' distance. The entire population followed them. They watched the Pleiades intently. If the world was to come to an end, if the sun was never to rise again, the Pleiades would not pass the zenith; but the moment they passed it, it was known that a new era of fifty-two years had been guaranteed to men. Fire was kindled anew by the friction of wood. But the wood rested on the bosom of the handsomest of the prisoners, and the moment it was lighted the victim's body was opened, his heart torn out, and both heart and body burned upon a pile that was lit by the new fire. No sooner did the people, who had remained on the plain below, perceive the flame ascend, than they broke into delirious joy. Another fifty-two years was before the world. More victims were sacrificed in gratitude to the gods. Brands were lighted at the sacred flame on the mountain, from which the domestic fires were in their turn kindled, and swift couriers were despatched with torches, replaced continually on the route, to the very extremities of the empire. It was in the year 1507, twelve years before

Cortes disembarked, that the Toxilmolpilia was celebrated for the last time. In 1559, although the mass
of the natives had meanwhile been converted to Roman
Catholicism, the Spanish government had to take
severe measures to prevent its repetition.[1]

We have far firmer footing, then, than is furnished
by the shifting ground of the cosmogonies, when we
insist upon the general prevalence of the feeling that
the world might veritably come to an end as it had
done before. Beyond this there was nothing fixed or
generally accepted. Much the same might be said of
the future life. The Mexicans believed in man's sur-
vival after death. This we see from the practice of
putting a number of useful articles into the tomb by
the side of the corpse, after first breaking them, so
that they too might die and their spirits might accompany that of the departed to his new abodes. They even
gave him some Tepitoton, or little household gods, to
take with him, and as a rule they killed a dog to serve as
his guide in the mysterious and painful journey which
he was about to undertake. Sometimes a very rich
man would go so far as to have his chaplain slaughtered, that he might not be deprived of his support in
the other world. But in all this there is nothing to
distinguish the Mexican religion from the beliefs that
stretched over the whole of America, and there is no

---

[1] See *Bancroft*, Vol. III. pp. 393—396

indication that any moral conception had as yet vivified and hallowed the prospect beyond the grave. The mass of ordinary mortals remained in the sombre, dreary, monotonous realm of Mictlan; for in Mexico, as in Polynesia, a really happy immortality was a privilege reserved for the aristocracy. There were several paradises, including that of Tlaloc, and above all the "mansion of the Sun," destined to receive the kings, the nobles and the warriors. There they hunt, they dance, they accompany the sun in his course, they can change themselves into clouds or humming-birds. An exception is made, however, irrespective of social rank, in favour of warriors who fall in battle and women who die in child-bed, as well as for the victims sacrificed in honour of the celestial deities and destined to become their servants. So, too, the paradise of Tlaloc, a most beauteous garden, is opened to all who have been drowned (for the god of the waters has taken them to himself), to all who have died of the diseases caused by moisture, and to the children who have been sacrificed to him. We recognize in these exceptions an unquestionable tendency to introduce the idea of justice as qualifying the desolating doctrine of aristocratic privilege; and probably this principle of justice would have become preponderant, here as elsewhere, had not the destinies of the Mexican religion been suddenly broken off. Nor is it easy to explain the asceticism and austerities of which we have spoken, except on the supposition that those who practised them all their lives believed they were thereby acquiring higher rights in the future life. It must be admitted, however, that it is not in its doctrine of a future life that the Mexican religion reached its higher developments.

We must postpone till we have examined the Peruvian religion, which presents so many analogies to that of Mexico, while at the same time differing from it so considerably, the final considerations suggested by the strange compound of beliefs, now so barbarous and now so refined, which we have passed in review. Spanish monks, as we all know, succeeded within a few years in bringing the populations who had submitted to the hardy conquerers within the pale of their Church. It was no very difficult task. The whole past had vanished. The royal families, the nobility, the clergy, all had perished. Faith in the national gods had been broken by events. The new occupants laid a grievous yoke upon the subject peoples, whom they crushed and oppressed with hateful tyranny; but we must do the Franciscan monks, who were first on the field in the work of conversion, the justice of testifying that they did whatever in them lay to soften the fate of their converts and to plead their cause before the Court of Spain. Nor were their efforts always unsuccessful. They were rewarded by the unstinted confidence and affection of the unhappy · natives, who found little pity or comfort save at the hands of the good Fathers. Let us add that many of the peoples, especially those from whom the human tithes of which we have spoken had been exacted by the Aztecs, were sensible of the humane and charitable aspects of a religion that repudiated these hideous sacrifices in horror, and raised up the hearts of the oppressed by its promises of a future bliss conditioned by neither birth nor social rank.[1]

But the worthy monks could not give what they had not got. And the religious education which they gave their converts reflected only too faithfully their own narrow and punctilious monastic spirit, itself almost as superstitious, though in another way, as what it supplanted. Nay, more: in spite of the best dispositions on either side, it was inevitable that the ancient habits and beliefs should long maintain themselves, though more or less shrouded beneath the new orthodoxy. In 1571, the terrible Inquisition of Spain came and established itself in Mexico to put an end to this state of things; and alas! it found as many heretics as it could wish to show that it had not come for nothing. And when the natives saw the fearful

[1] Compare the Appendix to Jourdanet's translation of Bernal Diaz, pp. 912 sqq.

tribunal at work, when the fires of the *autos-da-fé* were kindled on the plain of México and consumed by tens or hundreds the victims condemned by the Holy Office, do you suppose that the new converts felt well assured in their own hearts that the God of the Gospel was, after all, much better than Uitzilopochtli and Tezcatlipoca ?[1]

But we are stepping beyond the domain of history we have marked out for ourselves. The religion of Mexico is dead, and we cannot desire a resurrection for it. But the memory it has left behind is at once mournful and instructive. It has enriched history with its confirmatory evidence as to the genesis, the power and the tragic force of religion in human nature; and he who inspects its annals, now so poetical and now so terror-laden, pauses in pensive thought before the grotesque but imposing monument which thrills him with admiration even while he recoils with horror.

[1] On the conversion of the Mexicans, &c., compare the anonymous treatise at the end of *Kingsborough's* " Mexican Antiquities," Vol. IX. Cf. also *Torquemada*, Lib. XVII. cap. XX., Lib. XIX. cap. XXIX.

LECTURE IV.

PERU.—ITS CIVILIZATION AND CONSTITU-TION. THE LEGEND OF THE INCAS: THEIR POLICY AND HISTORY.

IV.

PERU.—ITS CIVILIZATION AND CONSTITU-
TION. THE LEGEND OF THE INCAS:
THEIR POLICY AND HISTORY.

WE pass to-day from North to South America; and
as in the former we confined ourselves to the district
which presented the Europeans of the sixteenth century with the unlooked-for spectacle of a native civilization and religion in an advanced stage of development, so in the latter we shall specially study that
other indigenous civilization, likewise supported and
patronized by a very curious and original religion,
which established itself along the Cordilleras on the
immensely long but comparatively narrow strip of
land between those mountains and the ocean. Peru,
like Mexico, was the country of an organized solar
religion; but the former, even more than the latter,
displays this religion worked into the very tissues of a
most remarkable social structure, with which it is so
completely identified as not to be so much as conceivable without it. The empire of the Incas is one of

the most complete and absolute theocracies—perhaps the very most complete and absolute—that the world has seen. But in order to get a clear idea of what the Peruvian religion was, we must first say a word as to the country itself, its physical constitution and its history.

The Peru of the Incas, as discovered and conquered by the Spaniards, transcended the boundaries of the country now so-called, inasmuch as it included the more ancient kingdom of Quito (corresponding pretty closely to the modern republic of Ecuador), and extended over parts of the present Chili and Bolivia. We learn from our ordinary maps that this whole territory was narrowly confined between the mountains and the sea. Observe, however, that it was nearly two thousand five hundred miles in length, four times as long as France, and that its breadth varied from about two hundred and fifty to about five hundred miles. From West to East it presents three very different regions. 1. A strip along the coast where rain hardly ever falls, but where the night dews are very heavy and the produce of the soil tropical. 2. The *Sierra* formed by the first spurs of the Cordilleras, and already high enough above the level of the sea to produce the vegetation of the temperate regions. Here maize was cultivated on a large scale, and great herds of vicunias, alpacas and llamas were pastured.

And here we may note a great point of advantage enjoyed by Peru over Mexico ; for the llama, though not very strong, serves as a beast of burden and traction, its flesh is well flavored and its wool most useful. 3. The *Montaña*, consisting of a region even yet imperfectly known, over which extend unmeasured forests, the home of the jaguar and the chinchilla, of bright-plumed birds and of dreaded serpents. Above these forests stretch the dizzy peaks and the volcanos. The most remarkable natural phenomenon of the country is the lake Titicaca, about seven times as great as the lake of Geneva, not far distant from the ancient capitol Cuzco, and serving, like Anahuac, the lake district of Mexico, as the chief focus of Peruvian civilization and religion. The mysterious disappearance beneath the ground of the river by which it empties itself, stimulated yet further the myth-forming imagination of the dwellers on its shores.

There is a remarkable difference between the ways in which the two civilizations of which we are speaking formed and consolidated themselves in Mexico and Peru respectively. We have seen that in Mexico the state of things to which the Spanish conquest put an end was the result of a long series of revolutions and wars, in which successive peoples had ruled and served in turn ; and the Aztecs had finally seized the hegemony, while adopting a civilization the origins of

which must be sought in Central America. In Peru
things had followed a more regular and stable course.
The dynasty of the Incas had maintained itself for
about six centuries as the patron of social progress
and of a remarkably advanced culture. Starting from
its native soil on the shores of Lake Titicaca, and long
confined in its authority to Cuzco and its immediate
territory, this family had finally succeeded in indefinitely extending its dominion between the mountains
and the sea, sometimes by successful wars and sometimes
by pacific means; for whole populations had more than
once been moved to range themselves of their own free
will under the sceptre of the Incas, so as to enjoy the
advantages assured to their subjects by their equitable
rule. When Pizarro and his companions disembarked
in Peru, the great Inca, Huayna Capac, had but recently
completed the empire by the conquest of the kingdom
of Quito.

It has been asked, which was the more marvellous
feat, the conquest of Mexico by Fernando Cortes, or
that of Peru by Pizarro. One consideration weighs
heavily in favor of Cortes. It is that he was the first.
When Francisco Pizarro threw himself with his handful of adventurers upon Peru in 1531, he had before
him the example of his brilliant precursor, to teach
him how a few Europeans might impose by sheer
audacity on the amazed and superstitious peoples; and

in many respects he simply copied his model. Like
him, he took advantage of the divisions and rivalries
of the natives ; like him, he found means of securing
the person of the sovereign, and was thereby enabled
to quell the subjects. On the other hand, he had even
fewer followers than Cortes. His company scarcely
numbered over two hundred men at first, and the
Peruvian empire was more compact and more wisely
organized than that of Mexico. We shall presently
see the principal cause to which his incredible success
must be ascribed ; but the net result seems to be, that
one hesitates to pronounce the feats of either adven-
turer more astounding than those of the other, especially
when we remember that Pizarro was without the political genius of Fernando Cortes, and was so profoundly
ignorant that he could not so much as read !

The family of the Incas, whose scourge Pizarro
proved to be, must have numbered many fine politicians in its ranks. Never has what is called a "dynastic
policy" been pursued more methodically and ably.
The proofs assail us at every moment. The Incas
were a family of priest-kings, who reigned, as children
of the Sun over the Peruvian land, and the Sun himself was the great deity of the country. To obey the
Incas was to obey the supreme god. Their person
was the object of a veritable cultus, and they had
succeeded so completely in identifying the interests of

their own family with those of religion, of politics and
of civilization, that it was no longer possible to distinguish them one from another. And yet it was this
very method, so essentially theoretic, of insisting on
the minute regulation of all the actions of human life
in the name of religion, which finally ruined the Incas.
Peru, in the sixteenth century, had become one enormous convent, in which everything was mechanically
regulated, in which no one could take the smallest
initiative, in which everything depended absolutely upon
the will of the reigning Inca ; so that the moment
Pizarro succeeded in laying hold of this Inca, this
" father Abbé," everything collapsed in a moment,
and nothing was left of the edifice constructed with
such sagacity but a heap of sand. And indeed this is
the fatal result of every theocracy, for it can never
really be anything but a *hierocracy* or rule of priests.
On the one hand it must be absolute, for the sovereign
priest rules in the name of God ; and on the other
hand it is fatally impelled to concern itself with every
minutest affair, to interfere vexatiously in all private
concerns (since they too affect religious ethics and
discipline), and to multiply regulations against every
possible breach of the ruling religion. It is a general
lesson of religious history that is illustrated so forcibly
by the fate of the Inca priest-kings.

I will not weary you in this case, any more than in

that of Mexico, with the enumeration of the authors
to whom we must go for information on the political
and religious history of the strange country with which
we are dealing. I must, however, say a few words
concerning a certain writer who long enjoyed the highest of reputations, and was regarded throughout the
last century as the most trustworthy and complete
authority in Peruvian matters. The Peruvians, far as
their civilization had advanced, in many respects, were
behind even the Mexicans in the art of preserving the
memory of the past; for they had not so much as the
imperfect hieroglyphics known to the latter. They
made use of *Quipus* or *Quipos*, indeed, which were
fringes, the threads of which were variously knotted
according to what they were intended to represent;
but unfortunately the Peruvians anticipated on a large
scale what so often happens on the small scale amongst
ourselves to those persons of uncertain memory who
tie knots on their handkerchiefs to remind them of
something important. They find the knot, indeed, but
have forgotten what it means! And so with the Peruvians. They were not always at one as to the meaning of their ancient Quipos, and there were several
ways of interpreting them. Moreover, after the conquest
the few Peruvians who might still have made some
pretension to a knowledge of them did not trouble
themselves to initiate the Europeans into their filiform

H

writing.   All that is left of it is the practice of the Peruvian women who preserve this method of registering the sins they intend to record against themselves in the confessional.[1]   Let us hope that they at least never experience any analogous infirmity to that which besets the knot-tiers amongst ourselves.[2]

[1] See *P. Pauke,* "Reise in d. Missionen von Paraguay:" Vienna, 1829, p. III.

[2] In addition to the works of *Acosta, Gomara, Herrera, Humboldt, Waitz* and *Müller,* already cited in connection with Mexico, and *Prescott's* "Conquest of Peru," we may mention the following authorities for the political and religious history of Peru:

Xeres (Pizarro's secretary): "Verdadera relacion de la conquista del Peru y provincia del Cuzco llamada la nueva Castilla . . . por Francisco de Xeres," &c.: Seville, 1534.   English translation by Markham in "Reports on the Discovery of Peru:" printed for the Hakluyt Society, London, 1872.—*Zarate* (official Spanish "auditor" in Peru): "Historia del descubrimiento y conquista del Peru. . . . La qual escriua Augustin de Carate," &c.: Antwerp, 1555.   English translation: "The strange and delectable History, &c.: translated out of the Spanish Tongue by T. Nicholas:" London, 1581.—*Cieza de Leon* (served in Peru for seventeen years): "Parte Primera Dela chronica del Peru," &c.: Seville, 1553.   The second and third Parts have never been printed.   English translation by Markham: Hakluyt Society, 1864.   [N. B. *Xeres* (or *Jeres*), *Cieza de Leon* and *Zarate,* are all contained in Tom. XXVI. of Aribau's "Biblioteca de autores Españoles."]—*Diego Fernandez* of Palencia (historiographer of Peru under the vice-royalty of Mendoza): "Primera, y Segunda Parte, de la Historia del Peru," &c.: Seville, 1571.—*Miguel Cavelo Balbor:* Historie du Pérou," in Ternaux-Compans, Vol. XV.—*Arriaga:* "Extir

To return to the Peruvian author of whom I
intended to speak. He is the celebrated Garcilasso

pacion de la Idolatria del Piru . . . Por el Padre Pablo Joseph de
Arriaga de la Compañia de Jesus : " Lima, 1621. Extracts are given
in Ternaux-Compans, Vol. XVII.—*Fernando Montesinos :* "Memoires
historiques sur l'Ancien Pérou : " translated from the Spanish MS. in
Ternaux-Compans, Vol. XVII. Montesinos rectifies Garcilasso de la
Vega on more points than one.—*Johannes de Laet :* "Novus Orbis,"
&c. : Leiden, 1633.—*Velasco :* "Historia del Reino de Quito," &c. :
Quito, 1844. This work is in three Parts, the second of which, the
"Historia Antigua," is the one referred to in future notes. This second
Part is translated in Ternaux-Compans, Vols. XVIII. XIX.

The Abbé *Raynal's* "Histoire philosophique et politique des étab-
lissements . . . des Européens dans les deux Indes" (10 vols. :
Geneva, 1770) made a great stir in its time, the English translation by
Justamond reaching a third edition in 1777; but it is now completely
forgotten, and has no real value for our purposes. I cannot refrain from
a passing notice of a romance which is now almost as completely forgotten as the Abbé Raynal's History, in spite of its long popularity : I
mean *Marmontel's* "Les Incas et la Destruction de l'empire du
Pérou : " Paris, 1777. The author derived his materials from Garcilasso de la Vega. In spite of the florid style and innumerable offences
against historical and psychological fact which characterize this work,
it cannot be denied that Marmontel has disengaged with great skill the
profound causes of the irremediable ruin of the Peruvian state.

Lacroix : "Pérou," in Vol. IV. of "L'Amérique" in "L'Univers
Pittoresque"—*Paul Chaix :* "Histoire de l'Amerique méridionale au
XVIe siècle," Part I. : Geneva, 1853.—*Wuttke :* "Geschichte des
Heidenthums," Theil I., 1852.—*J. J. von Tschudi :* "Peru. Reises-
kizzen aus den Jahren, 1838—1842 : " St. Gallen, 1846.— *Thos. J.
Hutchinson :* "Two years in Peru, with explorations of its Antiqui-

de la Vega, who published his *Commentarios reales* in
1609 and 1617.[1]   Garcilasso's father was a European,
but his mother was a Peruvian, and, what is more, a
Palla, that is to say, a princess of the family of the
Incas.   Born in 1540, this Garcilasso had received
from his mother and a maternal uncle a great amount
of information as to the family, the history and the
persons of the ancient sovereigns.   He was extremely
proud of his origin; so much so, indeed, that he
issued his works under the name of "Garcilasso *el*

ties;" London, 1873.   Hutchinson had good reason to point out the
exaggerations in which Garcilasso indulges with reference to his ancestors, the Incas, but he himself speaks too slightingly of their government.   Had it not been in the main beneficent and popular, it could
not have left such affectionate and enduring memories in the minds of
the native population.

For the method of citation, see end of note on p. 18.

[1] This work is in two Parts, the first of which (Lisbon, 1609) gives
an account of the native traditions, customs and history prior to the
Spanish conquest, while the second (published under the separate title
of *Historia General del Peru:* Cordova, 1617) deals with the Spanish
conquest, &c.   English translation by Sir Paul Rycaut: London, 1688,
not at all to be trusted; both imperfect (omitting and condensing in an
arbitrary fashion) and incorrect.   As it may be in the possession of some
of my readers, however, reference will be made to it in future notes.
The earlier and more important part of Garcilasso's work has recently
been translated for the *Hakluyt Society* by *Clements R. Markham,* 2
vols.: London, 1869, 1871.   References are to the *Commentarios
reales* (Part I.), unless otherwise stated.

Inca de la Vega," though he had no real title to the name of Inca, which could not be transmitted by women. A genuine fervour breathes through his accounts of the history of his Peruvian country and his glorious ancestors, and it is to him that we owe the knowledge of many facts that would otherwise have been lost. The interest of his narrative explains the reputation so long enjoyed by his work, but the more critical spirit of recent times has discovered that his filial zeal has betrayed him into lavish embellishments of the situation created by the clever and cautious policy of his forebears, the Incas. He has passed in silence over many of their faults, and has attributed more than one merit to them to which they have no just claim. But in spite of all this, when we have made allowance for his family weakness, we may consult him with great advantage as to the institutions and sovereigns of ancient Peru.

We must allow, with Garcilasso, that from the year 1000 A. D. onwards (for he places the origin of their power at about this date) the Incas had accomplished a work that may well seem marvellous in many respects. Had there been any relations between Peru and Central America? Can we explain the Peruvian civilization as the result of an emigration from the isthmic region, or an imitation of what had already been realized there? There is not the smallest trace of any

such thing. No doubt it would be difficult to justify
a categorical assertion on a subject so obscure; but it
is certain that when they were discovered, Peru and
the kingdom of Quito were separated from North
America by immense regions plunged in the deepest
savagery. Beginning at the Isthmus of Panama, this
savage district stretched over the whole northern portion of South America, broken only by the demi-civilization of the Muyscas or Chibchas (New Granada);
and the Peruvians knew nothing of the Mexicans.
Neither the one nor the other were navigators, and
nothing in the Peruvian traditions betrays the least
connection with Central America. The most probable
supposition is, that an indigenous civilization was
spontaneously developed in Peru by causes analogous
to those which had produced a similar phenomenon in
the Maya country. In Peru, as in Central America,
the richness of the soil, the variety of its products, the
abundance of vegetable food, especially maize, secured
the first conditions of civilization. The Peruvian
advance was further favoured by the fact that it was
protected towards the East by almost impassable
mountains, and towards the West by the sea, while to
the North and South it might concentrate its defensive
forces upon comparatively narrow spaces.

The whole territory of the empire was divided into
three parts. The first was the property of the Sun,

that is to say of the priests who officiated in his numerous temples; the second belonged to the reigning
Inca; and the third to the people. The people's land
was divided out every year in lots apportioned to the
needs of each family, but the portions assigned to the
Curacas, or nobles, were of a magnitude suited to their
superior dignity. Taxes were paid in days of labour
devoted to the lands of the Inca and those of the Sun,
or in manufactured articles of various kinds, for the
cities contained a number of artizans. Indeed, it was
one of the maxims of the Incas that no part of the
empire, however poor, should be exempt from paying
tribute of one kind or another. To such a length was
this carried, that so grave a historian as Herrera tells
us how the Inca Huayna Capac, wishing to determine
what kind of tribute the inhabitants of Pasto were to
pay, and being assured that they were so entirely without resources or capacity of any kind that they could
give him nothing at all, laid on them the annual tribute of a certain measure of vermine, preferring, as he
said, that they should pay this singular tax rather than
nothing.[1] We cannot congratulate the officials commissioned to collect the tribute, but we cite this sample
in proof of the rigour with which the Incas carried out
the principles which they considered essential to the

[1] *Herrera*, Decada v. Libro iv. cap. ii. (Vol. IV. p. 335, in Stevens's
epitomized translation).

government of the country. The special principle we have just illustrated was founded on the idea that the Sun journeys and shines for every one, and that accordingly every one should contribute towards the payment of his services. For the rest, the great herds of llamas, which constituted a regular branch of the national wealth, could only be owned by the temples of the Sun and by the Inca. Every province, every town or village, had the exact nature and the exact quantity of the products it must furnish assigned, and the Incas possessed great depôts in which were stored provisions, arms and clothes for the army, All this was regulated, accounted for and checked by means of official Quipos.

The numerous body of officials charged with the general superintendence and direction of affairs was organized in a very remarkable manner, well calculated to consolidate the Inca's power. All the officials held their authority from him, and represented him to the people, just as he himself represented the Sun-god. At the bottom of the scale was an official overseer for every ten families, next above an overseer of a hundred families, then another placed over a thousand, and another over ten thousand. Each province had a governor who generally belonged to the family of the Incas. All this constituted a marvellous system of surveillance and espionage, descending from the sovereign himself to the meanest of his subjects, and founded on the principle that the rays of the Sun pierce everywhere. The lowest members of this official hierarchy, the superintendents of ten families, were responsible to their immediate superiors for all that went on amongst those under their charge, and those superiors again were responsible to the next above them, and so on up to the Inca himself, who thus held the threads of the whole vast net-work in the depths of his palace. It was another maxim of the Peruvian state that every one must work, even old men and children. Infants under five alone were excepted. It was the duty of the superintendents of ten families to see that this was carried out everywhere, and they were armed with disciplinary powers to chastise severely any one who remained idle, or who ordered his house ill, or gave rise to any scandal. Individual liberty then was closely restrained. No one could leave his place of residence without leave. The time for marriage was fixed for both sexes—for women at eighteen to twenty, for men at twenty-four or upwards. The unions of the noble families were arranged by the Inca himself, and those of the inferior classes by his officers, who officially assigned the young people one to another. Each province had its own costume, which might not be changed for any other, and every one's birthplace was marked by a ribbon of a certain

6

colour surrounding his head.[1]　In a word, the Jesuits
appear to have copied the constitution of the Peruvian
society when they organized their famous Paraguay
missions, and perhaps this fact may help us to trace
the profound motives which in either case suggested
so minutely precise a system of inserting individuals
into assigned places which left no room for self-
direction.　The Incas and the Jesuits alike had to
contend against the disconnected, incoherent turbu-
lence of savage life, and both alike were thereby
thrown upon an exaggerated system of regulations,
in which each individual was swaddled and meshed
in supervisions and ordinances from which it was
impossible to escape.

Having said so much, we must acknowledge that,
generally speaking, the Incas made a very humane
and paternal use of their absolute power.　They strove
to moderate the desolating effects of war, and generally treated the conquered peoples with kindness.　But
we note that in the century preceding that of the
European conquest, they had devised a means of
guarding against revolts exactly similar to the measures enforced against rebellious peoples by the des-
potic sovereigns of Nineveh and Babylon; that is to
say, they transported a great part of the conquered

---

[1] *Garcilasso,* Lib. iv. cap. viii., Lib. v. capp. vii. viii. xiii.; *Acosta,*
Lib. vi. capp. xiii. xvi.; *Montesinos,* p. 57.

populations into other parts of their empire, and it appears that Cuzco, like Babylon, presented an image in miniature of the whole empire. There, as at Babylon, a host of different languages might be heard, and it was amongst the children of the deported captives that Pizarro, like Cyrus at Babylon, found allies who rejoiced in the fall of the empire that had crushed their fathers. For the rest, the Incas endeavoured to spread the language of Cuzco, the *Quechua*, throughout their empire.[1] Nothing need surprise us in the way of political sagacity and insight on the part of this priestly dynasty. Its monarchs seem to have hit upon every device which has been imagined elsewhere for attaching the conquered peoples to themselves or rendering their hostility harmless. Thus you will remember that at Mexico there was a chapel that served as a prison for the idols of the conquered. In the same way there stood in the neighborhood of Cuzco a great temple with seventy-eight chapels in it, where the images of all the gods worshipped in Peru were assembled. Each country had its altar there, on which sacrifice was made according to the local customs.[2]

---

[1] *Garcilasso*, Lib. vi. cap. xxxv.

[2] *Garcilasso*, Lib. v. cap. xii.; *Herrera*, Dec. v. Lib. iv. cap, iv. (Vol. IV. p. 344, in Stevens's translation). See also *Hazart*, "Historie van Peru," Part II. chap. iv.; in his "Kerckelijcke Historie van de Gheheele Wereldt," Vol. I. p. 315 : Antwerp, 1682.

The Spaniards, amongst whom respect for the royal person was sufficiently profound, were amazed by the marks of extreme deference of which the Inca was the object. They could not understand at first that actual religious worship was paid to him. He alone had the inherent right to be carried on a litter, and he never went out in any other way, imitating the Sun, his ancestor, who traverses the world without ever putting his foot to the ground. Some few men and women of the highest rank might rejoice in the same distinction, but only if they had obtained the Inca's sanction. In the same way, it was only the members of the Inca family and the nobles of most exalted rank who were allowed to wear their hair long, for this was a distinctive sign of the favourites of the Sun. None could enter the presence of the reigning Inca save barefooted, clad in the most simple garments and bearing a burden on his shoulders, all in token of humility; nor must he raise his eyes throughout the audience, for no man looks upon the face of the Sun. It seems that the Incas possessed " the art of royal majesty" in a high degree. They could retain the impassive air of indifference, whatever might be going on before their eyes, like the Sun, who passes without emotion over everything that takes place below. It was thus that Atahulapa appeared to the Spaniards, who remarked the all but stony fixity of the Peruvian

monarch's features in the presence of all the new
sights—horses, riding, fire-arms—which filled his subjects with surprise and terror.[1]   And such was the
superhuman character of the Inca, that even the base
office of a spittoon—excuse such a detail—was supplied
by the hand of one of his ladies.[2]   The salute was
given to the Inca by kissing one's hand and then
raising it towards the Sun.   At his death the whole
country went into mourning for a year.   The young
Incas were educated together, under conditions of
great austerity, and were never allowed to mingle with
young people of the inferior classes.[3]

The army of the Incas was the army of the Sun.
The obligation to military service was universal, since
the Sun shines for all men.   Every sound man from
twenty-five to fifty might be called on to serve in his
company.   Thus numerous and highly-disciplined
armies were raised, for the spirit of obedience had penetrated all classes of the people.   The Incas had abol-
ished the use of poisoned arrows, which is so common
amongst the natives of the New World.[4]

Justice was organized after fixed laws, and, as is

---

[1] See *Gomara* (in Vol. XXII. of the Bibliotheca de Autores Españoles), p. 228 a; *Garcilasso*, " Historia General," &c., Lib. i. cap. xviii.;
cf. *Prescott*, Bk. iii. chaps. v. vi., and Appendices viii. ix.

[2] *Gomara*, p. 232 a.   [3] Cf. *Waitz*, Theil IV. S. 411, 418.

[4] Cf. *Garcilasso*, Lib. v. cap. xiii.; *Prescott*, Bk. i. chap. ii.

usually the case in theocracies, these laws were severe. For in theocracies, to the social evil of the offence is added the impiety committed against the Deity and his representative on earth. The culprit has been guilty not only of crime, but of sacrilege. The penalty of death was freely inflicted even in the case of offences that implied no evil disposition.[1] The palanquin-bearer, for instance, who should stumble under his august burden when carring the Inca, or any one who should speak with the smallest disrespect of him, must die. But we must also note certain principles of sound justice which the Incas had likewise succeeded in introducing. The judges were controlled, and, in case of unjust judgments, punished. The law was more lenient to a first offence than to a second, to crimes committed in the heat of the moment than to those of malise prepense; more lenient to children than to adults, and (mark this) more lenient to the common people than to the great.[2] The members of the Inca family alone were exempted from the penalty of death, which in their case was replaced by imprisonment for life. They alone might, and indeed must, marry their

---

[1] *Müller*, p. 406.

[2] See *Herrera*, Dec. v. Lib. iv. cap. iii. [Vol. IV. pp. 337 sqq. in Stevens's translation]; *Garcilasso*, Lib. ii. capp. xii. xiii. xiv. [p. 35 of Rycaut's translation, in which the passage is much shortened], Lib. v. cap. xi.; *Velasco*, Lib. ii. § 6.

sisters, for a reason that we shall see further on. Thus everything was calculated to set this divine family apart. Polygamy, too, was only allowed to the Incas and to the families of next highest rank after them, who, however, might not marry at all without the personal assent of the sovereign.[1] But the Incas strove to make themselves loved. Herrera tells us of establishments in which orphans and foundlings were brought up at the Inca's charges, and of the alms he bestowed on widows who had no means of subsistence.[2]

The same deliberate system shows itself in the attempts to spread education. The Incas founded schools, but they were opened only to the children of the Incas and of the nobility. This is a genuine theocratic trait. Garcilasso tells us naively that his ancestor the Inca Roca (1200—1249) in founding public schools had no idea of allowing *the people* " to get information, grow proud, and disturb the state."[3] The instruction, which was given by the *amautas* (sages), turned on the history or traditions of the country, on the laws, and on religion. We have said

---

[1] *Acosta*, Lib. vi. cap. xviii.; *Herrera*, Dec. v. Lib. iv. cap. i. and end of cap. iii. [Vol. IV. pp. 329 sq., 342, in Stevens's translation].

[2] *Garcilasso*, Lib. iv. cap. vii. ; *Herrera*, Dec. v. Lib. iv. capp. ii. iii. [Vol. IV. pp. 334, 341, in Stevens's translation] ; cf. *Montesinos*, p. 56.

[3] *Garcilasso*, Lib. iv. cap. xix.; cf. Lib. viii. cap. viii. (ad fin.)

that writing was unknown.　There were only the mnemonic Quipos, pictures on linen representing great events, and some rudimentary attempts at hieroglyphics which the Incas do not seem to have encouraged.　Indeed, there is reason to believe that the hieroglyphics found graven on the rocks of Yonan are anterior to the Inca supremacy;[1] and it is said that a certain *amauta* who had attempted to introduce a hieroglyphic alphabet, was burned to death for impiety at the order of the Inca.[2]

The most remarkable results of the rule of the Incas are seen in the material well-being which they secured to their people.　All the historians speak of the really extraordinary perfection to which Peruvian agriculture had been carried, though the use of iron was quite unknown.　The solar religion fits perfectly with the habits of an agricultural people, and the Incas thought it became them, as children of the Sun, to encourage the cultivation of the soil.　They ordered the execution of great public works, such as supporting walls to prevent the sloping ground from being washed away ; irrigation canals, some of which measured five hundred miles, and which were preserved with scrupulous care ; magazines of guano, the fertilizing virtues of which were known in Peru long before

[1] Cf. *Tschudi*, Vol. II. p. 387; *Hutchinson*, Vol. II. pp. 175-6.

[2] *Montesinos*, p. 119, cf. pp. 33, 108.

they were learned in Europe.[1]   The Spaniards are far from having maintained Peruvian agriculture at the level it had reached under the Incas.   Splendid roads stretched from Cuzco towards the four quarters of heaven; and Humboldt still traced some of them, paved with black porphyry, or in other cases cemented or rather macadamized, and often launched over ravines and pierced through hills with remarkable boldness.[2]   The Incas had established reservoirs of drinking water for the public use from place to place along these roads, and likewise pavilions for their own accommodation when they were traversing their realms, on which occasions they never travelled more than three or four leagues a day.   Bridges were thrown across the rivers, sometimes built of stone, but more often constructed on the method, so frequently described, that consists in uniting the opposing banks by two parallel ropes, along which a great basket is slung.[3]   A system of royal courier posts measured the great roads as in Mexico.   There were many important cities in Peru, and, according to a contemporary estimate cited by Prescott, the capital, Cuzco, even without including its suburbs, must have embraced at least two hundred thousand inhabitants.[4]   Architecture was in a developed stage.   We shall have to speak of the temples pres-

---

[1] *Garcilasso*, Lib. v. cap. iii.   [2] *Humboldt*, pp. 108, 294.

[3] *Gomara*, p. 277 b.   [4] *Prescott*, Bk. iii. chap. viii.

I   6*

ently.   The Inca's palaces—and there was at least one
in every city of any importance—were of imposing
dimensions, and a high degree of comfort and luxury
was displayed within them.   Gold glittered on the walls
and beneath the roofs, which were generally thatched
with straw.   They were provided with inner courts,
spacious halls, sculptures in abundance, but inferior, it
would seem, to those of Central America, and baths
in which hot or cold water could be turned on at will.[1]
In a word, when we remember from how many resources
the Peruvians were still cut off by their ignorance and
isolation, we cannot but admit that a genuine civilization is opening before our eyes, the defects of which
must not blind us to its splendour.   And since this
civilization was in great part due (we shall see the
force of the qualification presently) to the continuous
efforts of the Incas, our next task must be to ascend
to the mythic origin of that family, which we borrow
from the narrative of their descendant, Garcilasso de
la Vega.[2]

Properly speaking, this narrative is the local myth
of the Lake Titicaca and Cuzco, transformed into an
imperial myth.

Before the Incas, we are told, men lived in the most

---

[1] Cf. *Garcilasso*, Lib. vi. cap. iv.

[2] *Garcilasso*, Lib. i. capp. ix.—xvii.; cf. Lib. ii. cap. ix., Lib. iii. cap.
xxv.

absolute savagery. They were addicted to cannibalism, and offered human victims to gods who were gross like themselves. At last the Sun took pity on them, and sent them two of his children, Manco Capac and Mama Ogllo (or Oullo, Ocollo, Oolle, &c.), to establish the worship of the Sun and alleviate their lot. The two emissaries, son and daughter of the Sun and Moon, rose one day from the depths of the Lake Titicaca. They had been told that a golden splinter which they bore with them would pierce the earth at the spot in which they were to establish themselves, and the augury was fulfilled on the site of Cuzco, the name of which signifies *navel*.[1] Observe that, in classical antiquity, Babylon, Athens, Delphi, Paphos, Jerusalem, and so forth, each passed for the navel of the earth. Manco Capac and Mama Ogllo, then, established the worship of the Sun. They taught the savage inhabitants of the place agriculture and the principal trades, the art of building cities, roads and aqueducts. Mama Ogllo taught the women to spin and weave. They appointed a number of overseers to take care that every one did his duty; and when they had thus regulated everything in Cuzco, they re-ascended to heaven. But they left a son and

[1] Such at least is the etymology proposed by Garcilasso (Lib. i. cap. xviii.). Modern Peruvian scholars rather incline to refer *Cuzco* to the same root as *cuzcani* ("to clear the ground").

daughter to continue their work. Like their parents, the brother and sister became husband and wife, and from them descends the sovereign family of the Incas, that is to say, the Lord-rulers, or Master-rulers.

Such is the legend, from which the first deduction must be that the Inca family has nothing in common with the other denizens of earth. It is super-imposed, as it were, on humanity. It is because of this difference of origin that the laws which restrain the rest of mankind are not always applicable to the Incas. For example, they marry their sisters, as Manco Capac did, and as the Sun does, for the Moon is at once his wife and his sister, It is thus that they are enabled to preserve the divine character of their unique family.

For ourselves, we can entertain no doubt that this is a cosmic myth. Mama Ogllo, or " the mother egg," and Manco Capac, or " the mighty man," are two creators. The myth indicates that there existed an ancient solar priesthood on one of the islands or on the shores of the Lake of Titicaca (at an early date the focus of a certain civilization), and that this priestly family became at a given period the ruling power at Cuzco. It was thence that it radiated over the small states which surrounded Cuzco, embracing them one after another under its prestige and its power, until it had become the redoubtable dynasty that we know it. Manco Capac and Mama Ogllo, the creator and the cosmic egg, have become the Sun and Moon, represented by their Inca high-priest and his wife. There is no practice towards which a more wide-spread tendency exists in America than that of conferring the name of a deity on his chief priest. And if Garcilasso fixes the appearance of Manco Capac at about 1000 A. D., it is simply because the historical recollections of his family mounted no higher, and that about that time it began to rise out of its obscurity. It had the advantage of numbering in its royal line both successful warriors and, what is more, consummate politicians, instances of whose ability we have already seen and shall see again.

The point at which the legend preserved by Garcilasso is clearly at fault, is in its claim for the Incas as the first and only civilizers of Peru. We shall presently meet with other Peruvian myths of civilization which do not stand in the least connection with Manco Capac and the Incas. The kingdom of Quito, which the Inca Huayna Capac had recently conquered when the Spaniards arrived, though not on the same level as Peru proper, was far removed from the savage state, while as yet a stranger to the influence of the Incas. The country of the Muyscas, the present New Granada or land of Bogota, though standing in no connection with Peru, was the theatre of another sacerdotal and solar religion *sui generis*, which though very little known, is highly interesting. The valley of the Rimac,

or Lima, and the coast lands in general, were likewise centres of a pre-Inca civilization. The Chimus
especially, themselves dwellers on the coast, were possessed of an original civilization differing from that of
the Incas. They were the last to be conquered. To
sum up, everything leads us to suppose that various
centres of social development had long existed, up and
down the whole region, but that, under the presiding
genius of the priesthood of Manco Capac, the civilization of Cuzco had gradually acquired the preponderance, till it consecutively eclipsed and absorbed all the
others.

Garcilasso labours hard to impress us with the belief
that the sovereigns of his family maintained an unbroken age of gold, by dint of their wisdom and virtues. But we know, both from himself and from
other sources, that as a matter of fact the Incas' sky
was not always cloudless. They had numbered both
bad and incapable rulers in their line. More than
once they had had to suppress terrible insurrections,
and their palaces had witnessed more than one tragedy.[1]

[1] See the critical summary of the history of the Incas in *Waitz*,
Theil. IV. S. 396 sq. The following table of the successive Incas
follows Garcilasso :

Manco Capac,	about 1000
Sinchi Roca,	died about 1091
Lloque Yupanqui	" 1126

But after making all allowances, we must admit that they succeeded in governing well, and more especially in maintaining intact their own religious and political prestige.

Now this very cleverness, this conscious and often extremely deliberate and astutely calculated policy, compels us to ask how far the Incas themselves were sincere in their pretension to be descended from the Sun, and their faith in the very special favour in which the great luminary held them. There is so much rationalism in their habitual tactics, that one cannot help suspecting a touch of it in their beliefs. And the truth is that their descendant, Garcilasso, has recorded certain traditions to that effect, which he has perhaps dressed up a little too much in European style, with a view to convincing us that his ancestors were mon-

Mayta Capac,	died about	1156
Capac Yupanqui,	"	1197
Inca Roca,	"	1249
Yahuar Huacac,	"	1289
Viracocha Inca Ripac	"	1340
[Inca Urco, who only reigned 11 days, is omitted by Garcilasso]		
Tito Manco Capac Pachacutec,	"	1400
Yupanqui,	"	1438
Tupac Yupanqui	"	1475
Huayna Capac,	"	1525
Huascar, ⎫	"	⎧ 1532
Atahualpa, ⎭	"	⎩ 1533

otheistic philosophers, but which nevertheless bear
the marks of a certain authenticity. For the reasoning
which Garcilasso puts into the mouth of the Incas
closely resembles what would naturally commend
itself to the mind of a pagan who should once ask
himself whether the visible phenomenon, the Sun,
which he adored, was really as living, as conscious, as
personal, as they said. Thus the Inca Tupac Yupanqui
(fifteenth century) is said to have reasoned thus :[1]

" They say that the Sun lives, and that he does everything.
But when one does anything, he is near to the thing he does;
whereas many things take place while the Sun is absent. It
therefore cannot be he who does everything. And again, if he
were a living being, would he not be wearied by his perpetual
journeyings ? If he were alive, he would experience fatigue,
as we do ; and if he were free, he would visit other parts of the
heavens which he never traverses. In truth, he seems like a
thing held to its task that always measures the same course, or
like an arrow that flies where it is shot and not where it wills
itself."

Note this line of reasoning, Gentlemen, which must
have repeated itself in many minds when once they
had acquired enough independence and power of
thought calmly to examine those natural phenomena

[1] *Garcilasso* Lib. viii. cap. viii. Garcilasso says that he translates
this passage, word for word, from the Latin MS. of the Jesuit Father,
Blas Valera.

which primitive naïveté had animated, personified and adored as the lords of destiny. Their fixity and their mechanical and unvarying movements, when once observed, could not fail to strike a mortal blow at the faith of which they were the object. That faith was transformed without being radically changed when it was no longer the phenomenon itself, but the personal and directing spirit, the genius, the deity that was behind the phenomenon, but distinct from it and capable of detaching itself from it, which drew to itself the worship of the faithful. But in his turn this god, shaped in the image of man, must either be refined into pure spirit, or must fall below the rational and moral ideal ultimately conceived by man himself. When all is said and done, Gentlemen, Buddhism is still a religion of Nature. It is the last word of that order of religions, and exists to show us that, at any rate in its authentic and primitive form, that last word is *nothingness.* And that is why Buddhism has never existed in its pure form as a popular religion. For in religion, and at every stage of religion, mind seeks mind. Without that, religion is nothing. Note, too, the observant Inca's remark, that if the Sun were alive he must be dreadfully tired. You may find the same idea in more than one European mythology, in which the Sun appears as an unhappy culprit condemned to a toilsome service for some previous fault; or,

again, an iron constitution is given him, to explain
why he is not worn out by his ceaseless journeying.

Now Tupac Yupanqui would not be the only Inca
who cherished a certain scepticism concerning his
ancestor the Sun. Herrera tells us that the Inca
Viracocha denied that the Sun was God;[1] and according to a story preserved by Garcilasso,[2] the Inca
Huayna Capac, the conqueror of Quito, who died
shortly after Pizarro's first disembarkment, must have
been quite as much a rationalist. One day, during
the celebration of a festival in honour of the Sun, he is
said to have gazed at the great luminary so long and
fixedly that the chief priest ventured on some respectful remarks to the effect that so irreverent a proceeding
must surprise the people. " I will ask you two questions," replied the monarch. " I am your king and
universal lord. Would any one of you have the
hardihood to order me to rise from my seat and take a
long journey for his pleasure? . . . And would the
richest and most powerful of my vassals dare to dis-
obey if I should command him on the spot to set out
in all speed for Chili?" And when the priest answered
in the negative, the Inca continued: "Then I tell you
there must be a greater and a more mighty lord above
our father the Sun, who orders him to take the course

---

[1] *Herrera*, Dec. v. Lib. iv. cap. iv. (Vol IV. p. 346, in Stevens's
translation.)   [2] Lib. ix. cap. x.

he follows day by day. For if he were himself the sovereign lord, he would now and again omit his journey and rest for his pleasure, even if he experienced no necessity for doing so."

Once more: I will not vouch for the exact form of these audacious speculations of the free-thinking Inca. But such reminiscences, collected independently by various authors, correspond to the conjectures forced upon us by the extreme political sagacity of the Incas. None but theocrats, in whose own hearts faith in their central principle was waning, could develop such astuteness and diplomacy. A sincere and untried faith has not recourse to so many expedients dictated by policy and the fear lest the joint in the armour should be found. It is to be presumed, however, that these heterodox speculations of the Incas themselves never passed beyond the narrow circle of the family and its immediate surroundings. Nothing of the kind would ever be caught by the ear of the people. But the evidence as to Huayna Capac's scepticism derives a certain confirmation from the fact that he was the first Inca who departed (to the woe of his empire, as it turned out) from some of the hereditary maxims that had always been scrupulously observed by his ancestors.

Huayna Capac had considerably extended the Peruvian empire by the conquest of the kingdom of Quito. In the hope, presumably, of consolidating his conquest, he resided for a long time in the newly-acquired territory, and married the conquered king's daughter, to whom he became passionately attached. This was absolutely contrary to one of the statutes of the Inca family, no member of which was allowed to marry a stranger. By his foreign wife he had a son called Atahualpa, and whether it was that he thought it good policy to allow a certain autonomy to the kingdom of Quito, or whether it was due to his tenderness towards Atahualpa's mother and the son she had borne him, certain it is that when he died at Quito in 1525, he decided that Atahualpa should reign over this newly-acquired kingdom, whilst his other son Huascar, the unimpeachably legitimate Inca, was to succeed him as sovereign of Peru proper. This, again, was a violation of the maxim that the kingdom of the Incas, which was the kingdom of the Sun, was never to be parted. It was in the midst of the struggles provoked by the hostility of the two brothers that Pizarro fell like a meteor amongst the Peruvians, who did not so much as know of the existence of any other land than the one they inhabited.

But the hour warns me that I must pause. When next we meet, I shall have to recount the fall of the great religious dynasty of the Incas, and we shall then examine more closely that Peruvian religion of which we have to-day but sketched the outline.

LECTURE V.

FALL OF THE INCAS.—PERUVIAN MYTHOLOGY. PRIESTHOOD.

141

V.

FALL OF THE INCAS.—PERUVIAN MYTHOLOGY. PRIESTHOOD.

I.

You will remember that when last we met we traced out the legendary origin of the royal house of the Incas. Starting from the shores of the Lake Titicaca and the city of Cuzco, and progressively extending its combined religious and political dominion over the numerous countries situated west of the Cordilleras, it had welded them into one vast empire, centralized and organized in a way that, in spite of its defects, extorts our admiration. You had occasion to notice the extraordinary degree to which the consummate practical sagacity which distinguished the sacerdotal and imperial family of the Sun for successive centuries, was combined with purely mythological principles of faith; and we were compelled to ask whether so much diplomacy was really consistent with unreserved belief. Finally we saw that, according to the historians, more than one of the Incas had in fact expressed and justified a doubt as to the living and conscious personality of that Sun-god whose descendants they were supposed to be. The position of affairs when the Spaniards disembarked on the shores of Peru is already known to you. The Inca Huayna Capac, conqueror of Quito, had broken with the constitutional maxims of his dynasty, in the first place by marrying a stranger, the daughter of a deposed king; and in the second place by leaving the kingdom of Quito to the son, Atahualpa, whom she bore him; while he allowed Huascar, the heir-apparent to the empire, to succeed him in Peru proper, thus severing into two parts the kingdom of the Sun, in defiance of the principle hitherto recognized, which forbad the division of that kingdom under any circumstances.

The war which speedily arose between Atahualpa and his half-brother, Huascar, was the great cause that made it possible for Pizarro and his miniature army to get a footing in the Peruvian territory. The military forces of both sections of the empire were engaged with each other far away from the place of landing, and the inhabitants, wholly unaccustomed to take any initiative, made no resistance to the strange invaders, whose appearance, arms and horses, struck terror into their hearts, and in whom (like the Mexicans in the case of Cortes and his followers) they thought they saw supernatural beings. Pizarro, who knew how things stood, had but one idea, viz., to imitate Cortes in laying hold of the sovereign's person. Atahualpa returned victorious. He had defeated Huascar, slaughtered many members of the Inca family, and thrown his conquered brother into prison, so as to govern Peru in his name, for he was not sure that he himself would be recognized and obeyed as a legitimate descendant of the Sun. Pizarro found means of making his arrival known to him, and at the same time offered him his alliance against his enemies.[1] Atahualpa was delighted with these overtures, and invited his pretended allies to a conference near Caxamarca, where the Spaniards had installed themselves. The Inca advanced, parading all the pomp and splendour of his solar divinity. Four hundred richly-clad attendants preceded his palanquin, which sparkled at a thousand points with gold and precious stones, and was borne on the shoulders of officers drawn from amongst the highest nobles, while troops of male and female dancers followed the child of the Sun and plied their art. Then ensued one of those unique scenes of history upon which, as indignation contends with amazement for the mastery in our minds, we must pause for a moment to gaze.

Pizarro's almoner, Father Valverde, drew near to

---

[1] *Herrera*, Dec. v. Lib. i. capp. ii. iii., Lib. iii. cap. xvii. (Vol. IV. pp. 240 sqq., 325 sqq., in Stevens's translation.)

K

the Inca, a crucifix in one hand and a missal in the other, and by means of an interpreter delivered a regular discourse to him, in which he announced that Pope Alexander VI. had given all the lands of America to the King of Spain, which he had a right to do as the successor of St. Peter, who was himself the Vicar of the Son of God. Then he expounded the chief articles of Christian orthodoxy, and summoned the Inca there and then to abjure the religion of his ancestors, receive baptism, and submit to the sovereignty of the King of Spain. On these conditions he might continue to reign. Otherwise he must look for every kind of disaster.

Atahualpa was literally stupefied. Much of the discourse, no doubt, he failed to follow, but what he did understand filled him with indignation. He answered that he reigned over his peoples by hereditary right, and could not see how a foreign priest could dispose of lands that were not his. He should remain faithful to the religion of his fathers, "especially," he added, as he pointed to the crucifix grasped by the monk, "since my god, the Sun, is at any rate alive; whereas the one you propose for my acceptance, as far as I gather, is dead." Finally, he desired to know whence his interlocutor had derived all the strange things that he had told him. "Hence!" cried Valverde, holding out his missal. The Inca, who had never seen a book in all his life, took this object, so new to him, in his hands, opened it, put it to his ear, and finding that it said nothing, flung it contemptuously on the ground.

Pizarro saw the moment for striking the blow he contemplated. Crying out at the sacrilege, he gave his soldiers the signal of attack. Their horses and fire-arms caused an instant panic. In vain did some of his officers attempt to defend the Inca. Pizarro broke through to him, seized him by the arm and dragged him to his quarters. All his escort fled in terror.

Atahualpa, then, was in the immediate power of Pizarro, who (still imitating Cortes) surrounded his prisoner with every comfort and attention, though confining him strictly to one chamber, and warning him that any attempt at escape or resistance would be the signal for his death. Atahualpa soon perceived that thirst for gold was the great motive that had impelled the Spaniards to their audacious enterprize. He hoped to disarm them by offering as ransom gold enough to fill the chamber in which he was confined up to the height of a man. He gave the necessary orders for collecting the precious metal in the requisite amount, and to secure the good reception of the emissaries whom Pizarro despatched everywhere to receive it. One of these detachments even entered into relations with the captive Inca, Huascar, and the latter hastened to offer the Spaniards yet more gold than Atahualpa was giving them if they would take his part. Atahualpa heard of this, was alarmed, regarded his conquered brother's attempts in the light of high treason, gave orders for his death—and was obeyed.[1]

He was not aware how precarious was his own tenure of life. Pizarro saw more and more clearly that, in order to become the real master of Peru, he must get rid of the reigning Inca, and put some child in his place, who would be a passive instrument in his hands. He was fairly alarmed by the religious obedience, timid but absolute, that the "child of the Sun," even in his captivity, received from all classes of his subjects. He fancied that from the recesses of his prison, and even while paying off his enormous ransom,[2] Atahualpa had sent secret orders to the most distant populations to arm themselves and come to his rescue. The interpreter through whom he communicated with his captive was out of temper

---

[1] *Herrera*, Dec. v. Lib. iii. cap. ii. (Vol. IV. p. 266, in Stevens's translation); *Gomara*, p. 231 a.

[2] In the course of a few months, Pizarro amassed such immense wealth that, after deducting the *fifth* for the king and a large sum for the reinforcements brought him by Almagro, he was still able to give £4000 to each of his foot-soldiers, and double that sum to each horseman. The calculation is made by Robertson, who estimates the *peso* at a pound sterling. To obtain the equivalent purchasing power in our own times, these sums would have to be more than quadrupled!

with his master, for his head had been so turned by
ambition, that he had demanded the hand of a *coya*,
that is to say, one of the Inca's women, and had been
haughtily refused. In revenge he made malicious
reports to Pizarro. But it was an accidental circumstance that brought the latter's ill-will towards his captive to a point. The Inca greatly admired the art of
writing when he discovered all the uses the Spaniards
made of it. One day it occurred to him to get one of
the soldiers on guard over him to write the word *Dio*
upon his nail, and he was delighted and astonished to
find that every one to whom he showed it read it in
the same way. So they told him that every one a little above the common herd could read and write in
Europe. His evil star would have it that he showed
his thumb one day to Pizarro, who could make nothing of it. Pizarro, then, could not read! Atahualpa
concluded that he was merely one of the common
herd, and found an opportunity of telling him so.
Pizarro, stung to the quick, hesitated no longer. A
mock judgment condemned Atahualpa to the extreme
penalty for the crimes of idolatry, polygamy, usurpa-
tion, fratricide and rebellion. In vain he appealed to
the King of Spain. He was led to the stake, and
Father Valverde made him purchase by a baptism *in
extremis* the privilege of being strangled instead of
burned alive.

From this moment the fate of Peru was decided. The head once struck from the great body, long convulsions ensued, but no serious resistance was possible. Pizarro set up as Inca a young brother of Huascar's, who was at first a mere instrument in the hands of his country's bleeders, but afterwards escaped and raised insurrections which ended in his total defeat. The Spaniards had been reinforced, and had found allies amongst the peoples who had been torn from their native soils by the victorious Incas.[1]   Other attempts, still attaching themselves to the name of some Inca, failed in like manner.   And yet the mass of the Peruvians, in spite of their conversion to Roman Catholicism, remained obstinately attached to the memory of their Incas.   One of their real or pretended descendants, in the eighteenth century, did not shrink from serving as a domestic at Madrid and Rome, as the only means of learning the secret of that European power which had so cruelly crushed his ancestors.[2]   But on his return to Peru (1744 A. D.) his efforts only ended in his destruction.   But this did not prevent a certain Tupac Amarou, who was descended from the Incas through a female line, from

---

[1] *Herrera*, Dec. v. Lib. viii. capp. i. sqq. (Vol. V. pp. 23 sqq. in Stevens's translation.)

[2] See *Alcedo*, " Diccionario Geográfico-Historico de las Indias Occidentales," &c.: Madrid, 1786-9: article *Chunchos*.

fomenting a rebellion in 1780, which it cost the Spaniards an effort to suppress.[1] Later on, after the revo-
lution that broke the bond of subjection to Spain, this
stubborn hostility of the Peruvians changed its character; but in 1867, Bustamente still tried to make capital out of the historical attachment of the natives
to the Incas by declaring himself their descendant.
The opposition, however, had long lost all vestige of
a religious character. The legend of Manco Capac,
which is still current amongst the people, has been
euhemerized. It is now no more than the story of a
just and enlightened prince, the benefactor of the
country. The natives, it seems, are fond of playing
a kind of drama, in which the trial and death of
Atahualpa are represented. Superstitious to the last
degree, they accept the practices of Catholicism with
a submission that has in it more of a melancholy and
hopeless resignation than an ardent or trusting faith.
The glorious age of the Incas is gone, and will never
return, but it is still regretted.[2]

II.

And now it is high time that we examined that reli-

---

[1] See *Waitz*, Vol. IV. pp. 477—497; *Tschudi*, Vol. II. pp. 346—
351; cf. *Castelnau*, "Expedition dans les Parties centrales de l'Amerique du Sud," &c.; Paris, 1850, &c., Part I. Vol. III. p. 282.

[2] *Tschudi*, ibid.

gion which was so closely associated with the whole
national life of Peru.

From all that I have said already, you will easily
understand that the Sun has never been worshipped
more directly or with more devotion than in Peru. It
was he whom the Peruvians regarded as sovereign
lord of the world, king of the heaven and the earth.
His Peruvian name was *Inti*, "Light." The villages
were usually built so as to look eastward, in order
that the inhabitants might salute the supreme god as
soon as he appeared in the morning. The most usual
representation of him was a golden disk representing a
human face surrounded by rays and flames. In Peru,
as everywhere else, a feeling existed that there was a
certain relation between the substance of gold and
that of the great luminary. In the nuggets torn from
the mountain sides they thought they saw the Sun's
tears.[1] The great periodic fêtes of the year, the imperial and national festivals in which every one took part,
were those held in honour of the Sun.

Immediately after him came his sister and consort
the Moon, Mama Quilla. Her image was a disk of
silver bearing human features, and silver played the
same part in her worship that gold did in that of the
Sun. It appears, however, that they performed fewer

---

[1] Cf. Spanish MS. cited by *Prescott*, Bk. i. chap. iii; *Velasco*, Lib. ii.
§ 4, sec. 15.

sacrifices to her than to her august consort, which is quite in harmony with the inferior position assigned to woman in the Peruvian civilization.[1] Like Selene amongst the Greeks, Mama Quilla, and her incarnation in human form, Mama Ogllo, were weavers. And that is why the latter was said to have taught the Peruvian women the art of spinning and weaving. This is a mythological conception suggested by likening the moonbeams to twisted threads, out of which, on fair clear nights, the brilliant verdure in which the earth is clad is spun.

But before going on to the gods who form the usual retinue of these two official and imperial deities, I must speak of two great Peruvian gods whose worship was likewise widely spread, but who nevertheless are not attached to the solar family, or at least are only so attached by an after-thought and by dint of harmonizing efforts which the Incas had their motives of policy for favouring: I mean the two great deities, *Viracocha* and *Pachacamac.*

The myth of Viracocha is the first instance we shall cite of traces of a certain civilization prior to the Incas, or at any rate of a belief widely spread in some parts of Peru that civilization had not really been, as the legend of the Incas would have it, the sole work of that sacerdotal family. The name of Viracocha

---

[1] *Prescott,* Bk. i. chap. iii.

7*

must be very ancient, for it became a generic name
to signify divine beings. It was given to Manco Capac
himself as a title of honour, and the Spaniards on
their arrival passed as *Viracochas* in the eyes of the
people. This name, according to Spanish authorities,
followed by Prescott,[1] signifies *Foam of the sea* or of
the *lake*. This would make the deity a male Aph-
rodite. He was represented with a long beard, and
human victims were sacrificed to him. At the same
time, they said that he had neither flesh nor bone,
that he ran swiftly, and that he lowered mountains
and lifted up valleys. The following legend was told
of him.[2]

There were men on the earth before the Sun
appeared, and the temples of Viracocha, for instance,
on the shores of Lake Titicaca, are older than the
Sun. One day Viracocha rose out of the lake. He
made the sun, the moon, the stars, and prescribed
their course for them. Then he made stone statues,
put life into them, and commanded them to go out
of the caverns in which he had made them and follow
him to Cuzco. There he summoned the inhabitants,
and set a man over them called Allca Vica, who was

---

[1] Cf. *Garcilasso*, Lib. v. cap. xxi., where the current etymology of the
word is rejected.

[2] See *Müller*, pp. 313 sqq, where all the views concerning him are
collected and discussed.

the common ancestor of the Incas. Then he departed and disappeared in the water.

Evidently this myth belongs to a different body of tradition from that of the Incas. When it says that the earth was peopled before the sun appeared, it is only a mythical way of asserting that there were men and even cities in Peru before the establishment of Sun-worship by the Incas. Now the latter claimed direct descent from the Sun, the supreme god, and they would not have readily allowed that this supreme deity had been made by another. One is rather tempted to find in this myth the echo of the claims put forward, with equal resignation and persistency, by a priesthood of Viracocha, that bowed its head before the supremacy acquired by the solar priesthood, but insisted all the same upon the fact that it was itself its elder brother.

But to what element can we affiliate the god Viracocha himself?

His aquatic name, *Foam of the sea* or *lake*, in itself leads us to suppose that he was closely related to the water. The supposition is confirmed by the saying that he had neither flesh nor bone, and yet ran swiftly. We can understand, too, why he lowers mountains and raises valleys. He rises from the water and disappears in it. He is bearded, like all aquatic gods, with their fringes of reeds. Finally, his consort and sister

Cocha is the lake itself, and also the goddess of rain. An old Peruvian hymn that was chanted under the Incas, and has fortunately been preserved, raises the character we have assigned to Viracocha above all doubt.[1] The goddess Cocha is represented as carrying an urn full of water and snow on her head. Her brother Viracocha breaks the urn, that its contents may spread over the earth. Here is the hymn, which is composed in nineteen short verses or lines :

1. Fair Princess,
3. Thy urn
2. Thy brother
4. Shatters.
5. At the blow
6. It thunders, lightens
7. Flashes ;
8. But thou, Princess,
10. Rainest down
9. Thy waters.
11. At the same time
12. Hailest,
13. Snowest.
14. World-former,
15. World-animator,
16. Viracocha,
17. To this office
18. Thee has destined,
19. Consecrated.

[1] This hymn was found by *Garcilasso* (See Lib. ii. cap. xvii., pp. 50, 51, in Rycaut's translation) among the papers of Father *Blas Valera*, and has been freed by *Tschudi* from the misprints, &c., that disfigured it in the printed editions of Garcilasso and all subsequent reproductions. See *Tschudi*, Vol. II. p. 381.

It admits of no doubt, therefore, that Viracocha
held a place in the Peruvian Pantheon closely analogous to that of Tlaloc, the rain-god, in its Mexican
counterpart. The blow with which he breaks his
sister's urn is the thunder-stroke. Inasmuch as rain
is a fertilizing agent, Viracocha represents its gene-
rative force. His resemblance to Tlaloc extends to
his demand for human victims, in which he is less
ferociously insatiable, but quite as pronounced, as
his Mexican analogue. Since his legend makes him
rise out of the Lake of Titicaca, we must think of
him as the chief god of the religion in honour before
that of the Incas rose to supremacy. When it is
said that after accomplishing his task he disappeared,
we are reminded that the river Desaguadero, which
carries off the waters of Lake Titicaca, sinks into the
earth and is lost to sight.

But there was yet another great deity, whose pretensions the Incas had allowed by making room
for him in the official religion, although he really
belonged to a totally different group of mythical
formations: I refer to Pachacamac, whose name
signifies " animator of the earth " from *caman*, " to
animate," and *pacha*, " earth."[1] The primitive centre
of his worship was in the valley of Lurin, south of
Lima, as well as in that valley of Rimac which has

[1] *Johannes De Laet*, Lib. x. cap. i. (p. 398, ll. 51, 52).

given its name to the city of Lima itself, for the latter is but a transformation of *Rimac*. It was there that Pachacamac's colossal temple rose. It was left standing by the Incas, but is now in ruins.[1] The branch of the Yuncas who resided there were already possessed of a certain civilization when the Inca Pachacutec annexed their country, at the close of the fourteenth century, partly by persuasion and partly by terror. Pachacamac was the divine civilizer who had taught this people the arts and crafts.[2] It would even seem that he had supplanted a still more ancient worship of Viracocha in these same valleys, for it is said that the latter was worsted in war by him and put to flight, upon which the new god renewed the world by changing the people he found on the earth into jaguars and monkeys, and creating a new and higher race. This opposition to Viracocha, god of the waters, puts us on the traces of Pachacamac's original significance. He must have been a god of fire, and especially of the internal fire of the earth, which displays itself in the volcanos and warms the spirit of man. He was a kind of Peruvian Dionysus. There was something gloomy and violent about his worship. He demanded human victims. The valley of Rimac really means the valley of the *Speaker*, of

---

[1] *Prescott*, Bk. i. chap. i.; *Garcilasso*, Lib. vi. cap. xxx.
[2] *Gomara*, p. 233 a; *Velasco*, Lib. ii. § 2, sec. 4.

him who answers when questioned. There was a kind of oracle inspired by the god of internal fire there. A certain feeling of mystery, as though in Pachacamac they had to do with a god less visible, less palpable, more spiritual than the rest, seems to have impressed itself upon his Peruvian worshippers. Garcilasso, who perhaps exaggerates a little, here as elsewhere, goes near to making him a god who could only be adored in the heart, without temple and without sacrifices.[1]

Thus, if the myth of Viracocha, god of the waters, makes the stars and the earth rise out of the moist element which he has fertilized and organized, the myth of Pachacamac makes him a kind of demiurge working within to form the world and enlighten mankind. I need not stay to point out what close analogies these two conceptions find in several of the cosmogonies of the Old World.

This confusion and rivalry of the Peruvian gods has left its traces in the crude and obscure legend of the Collas, or mountaineers of Pacari Tambo, to the south-west of Cuzco. "From the caves of Pacari Tambo (i. e. 'the house of the dawn') issued one day four brothers and four sisters. The eldest ascended a mountain, and flung stones towards the four cardinal points, which was his way of taking possession of all

[1] *Garcillasso* Lib. ii. capp. ii. iii.

the land. This aroused the displeasure of the other three. The youngest of all was the cunningest, and he resolved to get rid of his three brothers and reign alone. He persuaded his eldest brother to enter a cave, and as soon as he had done so closed the mouth with an enormous stone, and imprisoned him there for ever." This seems to refer to the quasi-subterranean cultus of Pachacamac, the internal fire, the first revelation of whom must have been a volcano hurling stones in every direction.—" The youngest brother then persuaded the second to ascend a high mountain with him, to seek their lost brother, and when they stood on the summit he hurled him down the precipice and changed him into a stone by a spell." I cannot say to what special deity this part of the legend alludes, unless it simply refers to an ancient worship of stones or rocks, many vestiges of which remained under the Incas, though it ceased to have any official importance in presence of the radiant worship of the Sun promulgated and favoured by the ruling family.—" Then the third brother fled in terror." This fleeing god must be Viracocha, the god of showers, who flees before the Sun.—" Then the youngest brother built Cuzco, caused himself to be adored as child of the Sun under the name of Pirrhua Manco, and likewise built other cities on the same model."[1]

---

[1] See *Montesinos*, pp. 3 sqq., whose version of the legend has been

This last trait puts it out of doubt that the legend is really an attempt to explain how the religion of Manco Capac established at Cuzco had succeeded in eclipsing all others, owing to the superior skill of its priesthood. It is a formal confirmation of all that I have told you of the consummate art with which the Incas gradually extended the circle of their political and religious dominion. *Pirrhua* is the contraction of Viracocha, taken in the generic sense of "divine being." Pirrhua Manco was an alternative name of Manco Capac.

Of course, this legend was not officially received under the Incas. The latter, being unable or unwilling to abolish the worship of Viracocha and of Pachacamac, took up a far more conciliatory attitude than that of the legends I have given. The supreme god, the Sun, was admitted to have had three sons, Kon or Viracocha, Pachacamac and Manco Capac; but the latter was declared to have been quite specially designed by the common father to instruct and govern men. By this arrangement every one was satisfied— and especially the Incas.

III.

We may now return to the other deities who were mainly followed in the text. Cf. however, for some of the details, *Garcilasso*, Lib. i. cap. xviii. (omitted by Rycaut); *Acosta*, Lib. i. cap. xxv. ; *Balboa*, pp. 4 sqq., &c.

L

officially incorporated in the family or retinue of the Sun.

The rainbow, *Cuycha*, was the object of great veneration as the servant of the Sun and Moon. He had his chapel contiguous with the temple of the Sun, and his image was made of plates of gold of various shades, which covered a whole wall of the edifice. When a rainbow appeared in the clouds, the Peruvian closed his mouth for fear of having all his teeth spoilt.[1]

The planet Venus, *Chasca* or the " long-haired star," so called from its extraordinary radiance, was looked upon as a male being and as the page of the Sun, sometimes preceding and sometimes following his master. The Pleiades were next most venerated. Comets foreboded the wrath of the gods. The other stars were the Moon's maids of honour.[2]

The worship of the elements, too, held a prominent place in this complicated system of nature-worship. For example, Fire, considered as derived from the Sun, was the object of profound veneration, and the worship rendered it must have served admirably as a link between the religion of the Incas and that of

---

[1] *Velasco,* Lib. ii. § 4, sec. 17; *Ph. H. Külb* in *Widenmann* and *Hauff's* " Reisen u. Länderbeshreibungen," Lief. xxvii.: Stuttgart, 1843, pp. 186–7.

[2] *Acosta,* Lib. v. cap. iv.; *Velasco,* Lib. ii. § 4, sec. 16; *Prescott,* Bk. i. chap. iii.; *Külb,* ibid.

Pachacamac. Strange as it may seem at first sight, the symbols of fire were stones. But our surprise will cease when we remember that stones were thought, in a high antiquity, to be animated by the fire that was supposed to be shut up within them, since it could be made to issue forth by a sharp blow. The Peruvian religion likewise adds its testimony to that of all the religions of the Old World, as to the importance which long attached to the preservation amongst the tribes of men of that living fire which it was so difficult to recover if once it had been allowed to escape. A perpetual fire burned in the temple of the Sun and in the abode of the Virgins of the Sun, of whom we shall have to speak presently. The wide-spread idea that fire becomes polluted at last and looses its divine virtue by too long contact with men, meets us once more. The fire must be renewed from time to time, and this act was performed yearly by the chief-priest of Peru, who kindled wood by means of a concave golden mirror. This miracle is very easy for us to explain, but we cannot doubt that the priests and people of Peru saw something supernatural in the phenomenon.[1]

The thunder, likewise, was personified and adored in certain provinces under the name of *Catequil*, but

---

[1] *Prescott*, ibid. In cloudy weather they had recourse to the method of friction.

it is a peculiarity of the Peruvian religion that it assigns a subordinate rank in the hierarchy to the god of thunder, who elsewhere generally takes the supreme place. In Peru, he was but one of the Sun's servants, though the most redoubtable of them all. The Peruvians are remarkable for their childish dread of thunder. A great projecting rock, often one that had been struck by the thunder passed for the deity's favoured residence. Catequil appears in three forms: *Chuquilla* (thunder), *Catuilla* (lightning), and *Intiallapa* (thunderbolt). His remaining name, *Illapa*, also means thunder. He had special temples, in which he was represented as armed with a sling and a club.[1] They sacrificed children, but more especially llamas, to him. Twins were regarded as children of the lightning, and if they died young their skeletons were preserved as precious relics. And, finally, we find in Peru the same idea that prevails in a great part of southern Africa, viz. that a house or field that has been struck by lightning cannot be used again. Catequil has taken possession of it, and it would be dangerous to dispute it with him.[2]

We have seen how the element of water was adored under the names of Viracocha and his sister Mama Cocha. The earth was worshipped in grottos or caves, often considered as the places whence men and gods

---

[1] *Prescott*, ibid.   [2] *Arriaga*, pp. 17, 32; *Külb*, ibid.

had taken their origin, and as giving oracles.[1]   There were also trees and plants that were clothed with a divine character, especially the esculent plants, such as the maize, personified as *Zarap Conopa*, and the potato, as *Papap Conopa*.   A female statue was often made of maize or coca leaves, and adored as the mother of plants.[2]

Thus we descend quite gently from the official heights of the religion of the Incas towards those substrata of religious thought which always maintain themselves beneath the higher religion that more or less expressly patronizes them, but to which they are not really bound by any necessary tie.   They are the survivals of old superstitions, to which the common people are often far more attached than they are to the exalted docrines which they are taught officially.   And it is thus, for example, that we note in Peru the very popular worship of numerous animals, mounting, without doubt, to a much higher antiquity than was reached by the religion of the Incas.   Indeed, I should be inclined to ascribe to the religious diplomacy of the children of the Sun the Peruvian belief which established a connection of origin between each kind of animal and a particular

---

[1] Cf. *Arriaga* pp. 10–17, &c. (cf. *Ternaux-Compans*, Vol. XVII. pp. 13, 14).

[2] *Acosta*, Lib. v. cap. v.; *Velasco*, Lib. ii. § 3, sec. 2; *Arriaga*, ibid.

star. The serpent, especially, seems to have been, in Peru as in Africa, the object of great veneration. We find it reproduced in wood and stone on an enormous number of the greater and smaller relics of Peruvian art. The god of subterranean treasures, *Urcaguay*, was a great serpent, with little chains of gold at his tail, and a head adorned with stag-like horns. The dwellers by the shore worshipped the whale and the shark. There were fish-gods, too, in the temple of Pachacamac, no doubt because of the enormous power of reproduction possessed by fishes. The condor was a messenger of the Sun, and his image was graven on the sceptre of the Incas.[1] It is remarkable that the llama does not appear amongst these divine animals, probably because it was so completely domesticated and wholly subject to man.

And finally, when we come to the *Guacas*, or *Huacas*, we reach the point where the Peruvian religion sinks into absolute fetichism.

The meaning of the word *Guaca*, or *Huaca*, was not very precise in the mouths of the Peruvians themselves. On the one hand, it was applied to everything that bore a religious character, whether an object of worship, the person of the priests, a temple, a tomb, or what not. The Sun himself was *Huaca*. The chief priest of Cuzco bore amongst other names that of

[1] *Tschudi*, Vol. II. pp. 396–7.

Huacapvillac, " he who converses with huaca beings."[1]
On the other hand, in ordinary language, this same
term was used to signify those wood, stone and metal
objects which were so abundant in Peru, of which we
still possess numerous specimens, and of which we
must now say a few words. Some of these huacas,
especially the stone ones, were of considerable size,
and no doubt dated from the pre-historic religion
before the Incas. But as a rule they were small and
portable, were private and hereditary property, and
were regarded as veritable fetiches, that is to say, as
the dwelling-places of spirits. Animism, in fact,
never ceased to haunt the imaginations of the Peruvians, especially amongst the lower orders, whether
the spirits were dreaded as malevolent sprites, or
courted as protectors and revealers. These huacas
represented (as true fetiches should) forms which were
sometimes animal, sometimes human, sometimes
simply grotesque, but always ugly and exaggerated.
Every valley, every tribe, every temple, every chief,
had a guardian spirit. Those which were analogous
to *pœnates publici* were recognized by the Incas, who
endowed them with flocks and various presents.
Often a stone in the middle of the village passed as the
abode of the patron spirit of the place. It was the
huacacoal, the stone of the huaca, whereas the huacas

[1] *Arriaga,* p. 18 (cf. *Ternaux-Compans,* Vol. XVII. p. 15).

of the family or house were distinguished as *conopas*.
Meteorites or thunderbolts were in great demand as
huacas, and especially amongst lovers, since they
were supposed to inspire a reciprocity of affection.
The Christian missionaries had more difficulty in
rooting out the worship of the Huacas than in abol-
ishing that of the Sun and Moon, and we may still
detect numerous traces of this ancient superstition
amongst the natives of Peru.[1]

IV.

Let us now turn to the priesthood which presided
over the worship of these numerous deities.

There was no sacerdotal caste in Peru, or, to speak
more correctly, the Inca family constituted the only
sacerdotal caste in the strict sense of the word.   This
family retained for itself all the highest positions in
the priesthood, as well as in the army and administra-
tion.   These priests of the higher rank bore special
garments and insignia, while the lower clergy wore
the ordinary costume.   At the head of all the priests
of the empire, first after the reigning Inca, stood the
Villac Oumau, " the chief sacrificer," also, as we have

---

[1] Cf. *Arriaga*, pp. 10–17 (cf. *Ternaux-Compans*, Vol. XVII. pp. 13,
14); *Acosta*, Lib. v. cap. v.; *Montesinos*, pp. 161-2; *Velasco*, Lib. ii. §
3, sec. 1.

seen, called the *Huacapvillac.* He was nominated by
the reigning Inca, and in his turn nominated all
his subordinates. His name indicates that he was
the living oracle, the interpreter of the will of the
Sun. You can understand, therefore, how important
it was for the policy of the Incas that he should
himself be subject to the authority and discretion
of the sovereign. After him came the rest of the
chief priests, also members of the Inca family, whom
he put in charge of the provincial temples of the
Sun. At Cuzco itself all the priests had to be Incas.
They were divided into squadrons, which attended
in succession, according to the quarters of the moon,
to the elaborate ritual of the service. And here we
must admire the consummate art with which the
Incas had planned everything in their empire to
secure their supremacy against all attaint, in religion
as in all else, while still leaving the successively
annexed populations a certain measure of religious
freedom. In the provinces, the Inca family, numerous as it was, could not have provided priests for
all the sanctuaries ; and, moreover, there would
be local rites, traditions, perhaps even priesthoods,
which could not well be fitted into the framework
of the official religion. The Incas therefore had
decided that the priests of the local deities should
be affiliated to the imperial priesthood, but in such

8

a way that the chief priests of the local deities should at the same time be subordinate priests of the deities of the empire. What a wonderful stroke of political genius! What happier method could have been found of teaching the subject populations, while still maintaining their traditional forms of worship, to regard the imperial cultus patronized by the reigning Inca as superior to all others? And what an invaluable guarantee of obedience was obtained by this association of the non-Inca priests with the official priesthood, the honours and advantages of which they were thus made to share, without any room for an aspiration after independence! I regard this organization of the priesthood in ancient Peru as one of the most striking proofs of the political genius of the Incas, and as one of the facts which best explain how a theocracy, which was after all based on the absolute and exclusive pretensions of one special mythology, was able to consolidate itself and endure for centuries, while exercising a large toleration towards other traditions and forms of worship.[1]

By the side of the priests there were also priestesses;

[1] On the priesthood, cf. *Arriaga*, pp. 17 sqq. [cf. *Ternaux-Compans*, Vol. XVII. p. 15]; *Prescott*, Bk. i. chap. iii.; *Balboa*, p. 29; *Velasco*, Lib. ii. § 3, sec. 8; *Garcilasso*, Lib. v. capp. viii. [ad fin.] xii. xiii.; *Müller*, p. 387; *Külb*, l. c. p. 187.

and they were clothed with a very special function. I refer to those *Virgins of the Sun* (*acllia*=chosen ones), those Peruvian nuns, who so much impressed the early historians of Peru. There were convents of these Virgins at Cuzco and in the chief cities of the empire. At Cuzco there were five hundred of them, drawn for the most part from the families of the Incas and the *Curacas* or nobles, although (for a reason which will be apparent presently) great beauty gáve even a daughter of the people a sufficient title to enter the sacred abode. They had a lady president—I had almost said a "mother abbess"—who selected them while yet quite young; and under her superior direction, matrons, or *Mamaconas*, superintended the young flock. They lived encloistered, in absolute retreat, without any relationship with the outside world. Only the reigning Inca, his chief wife, the *Coya*, and the chief priest, were allowed to penetrate this sanctuary of the virgins. Now these visits of the Inca's were not exactly disinterested. The fact is, that it was here he generally looked for recruits for his harem. You will ask how that could be reconciled with the vow of chastity which the maidens had taken; but their promise had been never to take any consort except the Sun, or *him to whom the Sun should give them.* Now the Inca, the child of the Sun, his representative and incarnation upon earth, began by assigning the most beautiful to himself, after which he might give some of those who had not found special favour in his eyes to his Curacas. And thus the vow was kept intact. In other respects, the most absolute chastity was sternly enforced. If any nun violated her vow, or was unhappy enough to allow the sacred fire that burned day and night in the austere abode to be extinguished, the penalty was death. And the strange thing is, that the mode of death was identical with that which awaited the Roman vestal guilty of the same offences. The culprit was buried alive. This illustrates the value of the theories started by those authors who can never discover any resemblance of rites or beliefs between two peoples without forthwith setting about to inquire which of the two borrowed from the other! It will hardly be maintained that the Peruvians borrowed this cruel custom from the ancient Romans, and assuredly the Romans did not get it from Peru. Whence, then, can the resemblance spring? From the same train of ideas leading to the same conclusion. By the sacrilege of the culprit, the gods of heaven and of light, the protecting and benevolent deities, were offended and incensed, and the whole country would feel the tokens of their wrath. To disarm their anger, its unhappy cause must expiate her guilt, and

at the same time must be removed from their sight
and given over to the powers of darkness, for she
was no longer worthy to see the light. And that
is why the dark tomb must swallow her. She had
betrayed her spouse the Sun—let her henceforth
be the spouse and the slave of darkness; and let
her be sent alive to those dark powers, that they
might do with her as they would. We must add
that the guilty nun's accomplice was strangled, and
that her whole family from first to last was put to
death.

The ordinary occupations of the Virgins of the
Sun consisted in making garments for the members
of the imperial family and tapestries destined to
adorn the temples and palaces, in kneading and
baking the sacred loaves, preparing the sacred drinks,
and, finally, in watching and feeding the sacred fire.
You perceive that it was not exactly the ascetic principle which had given rise to these convents—as
in the case of the Buddhist and Christian institutions, for example—but rather the desire to do honour
to the Sun, the supreme god, by consecrating serag-
lios to him, in which his numerous consorts, protected by a severe rule, could be kept from all except
himself and those to whom he might give them;
accomplishing, meanwhile, those menial tasks which,
especially under the rule of polygamy, woman

is required to perform in the abode of her lord and master.[1]

All this shows us once more, Gentlemen, how the same fundamental logic of the human mind asserts itself across a thousand diversities, and reappears under every conceivable form in every climate and every race. Only let us look close enough, and with the requisite information, and we shall find in every case that all is explained, that all holds together, that all is justified, by some underlying principle, and that " that idiot of a word," *chance*, is never anything but a veil for our ignorance. And thus when we notice anything paradoxical, grotesque, and unexplained by the resources we command at present, we must be very careful not to pronounce it inexplicable. We should rather suspend our judgment, wait till wider reflection and renewed investigation have shown us the middle terms, and meanwhile keep silence rather than attribute to chance or to influences which escape all human reason the phenomena that seem abnormal.

For instance, you have heard sometimes of the strange custom in accordance with which the father of a new-born child goes to bed and is nursed as an invalid. You are perhaps aware that this custom, that

[1] Cf. *Acosta*, Lib. v. cap. xv. ; *Montesinos*, p. 56 ; *Velasco*, Lib. ii. § 3, sec. 12, § 9, sec. 10 ; *Prescott*, Bk. i. chap. iii. and elsewhere.

appears so strange to us and is now restricted to a few savage tribes, was noted in ancient times in Europe itself, and has been preserved almost to our own time in certain cantons of the Pyrenees. It must therefore have been extremely wide-spread. Yet for a long time it seemed inexplicable. But now, thanks to investigations and comparisons, the explanation has been found. There is no doubt that the custom in question rested on the idea that there was a close solidarity between the health of the father and that of the new-born babe, so that if the father should fall sick, his far weaker child would die. The father, therefore, must be guarded from all over-exertion, must abstain from all excess—in short, was best in bed!

So, too, in the present case. How are we to explain the resemblance between the treatment of the Vestals at Rome and the Virgins of the Sun at Cuzco? It was once impossible, but now that we are better acquainted with the genesis, the spirit, the inner logic of the primitive religions, and the modes of life, the wants and the apprehensions proper to the pre-historic ages, we have no difficulty in attaching two parallel customs to a single religious principle which had found accept-ance alike in Italy and Peru. And this is one of the chief tasks, and one of the greatest charms, of the branch of study which I have the honour of professing. It shows us that even in human error, human reason has never abdicated its throne.

We have still to speak of the temples, the ritual and the chief festivals of ancient Peru. To these subjects we shall devote the first part of our sixth and last Lecture, reserving the closing portion for the conclusions and the general lessons suggested by our twofold study of Mexico and Peru.

LECTURE VI.

PERUVIAN CULTUS AND FESTIVALS.— MORALS AND THE FUTURE LIFE.—CONCLUSIONS.

PERUVIAN CULTUS AND FESTIVALS.— MORALS AND THE FUTURE LIFE.—CONCLUSIONS.

To complete my account of the native religion of Peru, I have still to speak of the cultus, the festivals, the religious ethics, and the ideas of a future life.

I.

The Peruvian cultus had given birth to the *temple;* and, indeed, it is highly interesting to witness what one may call the "genesis of the temple" on this soil, so different from those of the Old World. There were temples, indeed, before the Incas, but they differed both in style and in signification from those reared under their patronage. In Peru, as in Mexico, the temples were originally neither more nor less than extremely lofty altars; that is to say, artificial elevations, on the summit of which the sacrifices were presented, while a little chapel served to contain the image of the god or gods adored. Round this great

altar were grouped other chapels, galleries and columns, as though to accompany the great central altar
formed by the eminence itself. Under the Incas, the
crowning chapel increased so enormously that it encircled the altar and became the essential part of the
sacred structure.   The Inca temples were veritable
palaces, destined as abodes for the gods.   None of
them remain; but their ruins attest the fact that the
architects aimed rather at colossal than at beautiful
effects.   They contained gigantic stone statues, gates
cut out of monoliths, and the well-known pyramidal
structures of which we have spoken already.   The
most imposing of the temples was the one at Cuzco,
which consisted in a vast central edifice, flanked with
a number of adjacent buildings.   Gold was so pro-
digally lavished on its interior that it bore the name
of *Coricancha*, that is to say, "the place of gold."
The roof was formed by timber-work of precious
woods plated with gold, but was covered, as in the
case of all the houses of the land, with a simple thatch
of maize straw.   The doors opened to the East, and
at the far end, above the altar, was the golden disk of
the Sun, placed so as to reflect the first rays of the
morning on its brilliant surface, and, as it were, reproduce the great luminary.   And note that the mum-
mies of the departed Incas, children of the Sun, were
ranged in a semi-circle round the sacred disk on

golden thrones, so that the morning rays came day by day to shine on their august remains. The adjacent buildings were abodes of the deities who formed the retinue of the Sun. The principal one was sacred to the Moon, his consort, who had her disk of silver, and ranged around her the ancient queens, the departed *Coyas.* Others served as the abodes of Chaska, our planet Venus, the Pleiades, the Thunder, the Rainbow, and finally the officiating priests of the temple. In the provinces, the Incas reared a number of temples of the Sun on the model of that at Cuzco, but on a smaller scale.[1]

The Incas, however, had been anticipated in this striking development of the temple by the religions anterior or adjacent to their own. Witness the great temple of Pachacamac, which they left standing in the valley of Lurin, and the remarkable ruins of another great temple situated at some miles distance from Lake Titicaca, which has quite recently been made the subject of a careful reconstructive study by your compatriot Mr. Inwards.[2]

The offerings presented to the gods were very varied

---

[1] Cf. *Prescott,* Bk. i. chap. iii.; *Garcilasso,* Lib. iii. capp. xx.—xxiv.; *Paul Chaix,* Vol. I. pp. 249 sqq. On the temples of Pachacamac, which must have attained gigantic proportions before the time of the Incas, see *Hutchinson,* Vol. I. pp. 147—176.

[2] *Richard Inwards,* "The Temple of the Andes:" London, 1884.

in kind.   Flowers, fragrant incense, especially from
preparations of coca, vegetables, fruits, maize, prepared drinks offered in cups of gold.   At some of the
feasts the officiating priest moistened the tips of his
fingers in the cup and flung the drops towards the
Sun.   We also find in Peru a very special form of
that remnant of self-immolation which enters, in more
or less reduced and restricted shape, into the devotions
of so many peoples, and assumes such varied forms.
The Red-skin offers his sweat; the Black offers his
saliva or his teeth; the more poetical Greek, a lock
of his hair, or even all of it.   The Peruvian pulled
out a hair from his eyebrow and blew it towards the
idol![1]

But there were also sacrifices of blood.   A llama
was sacrificed every day at Cuzco.   Before setting out
on war, the Peruvians sacrificed a black llama that
they had previously kept fasting, that the heart of
their enemies might fail as did his.   This was the
Peruvian application of the principle that lies at the
base of all those superstitious ceremonies intended to
provoke or stimulate a desired effect by reproducing
its analogue in advance.   Small birds, rabbits, and, for
the health of the Inca, black dogs, were also sacrificed
frequently.   All these offerings were as a rule burned,

[1] *Acosta*, Lib. v. cap. xviii.; *Garcilasso*, Lib. ii. cap. viii. (p. 31 in
Rycaut), Lib. vi. cap. xxi,; *Arriaga*, p. 77.

that they might so be transmitted to the gods.[1] It should be noted that they only sacrificed edible animals,[2] which is a clear proof that the intention was to feed the gods. The sacrificing priest turned the animal's eyes towards the Sun, and opened its body to take out its heart, lungs and viscera, and offer them to the idols. It is a characteristic fact that when the victim was not burned, its flesh was divided amongst the sacrificers and *eaten raw*. The Peruvians had long learned to cook their meat, but this rite carries us back to a high antiquity, when cooking food was still an innovation which the power of tradition excluded from the ritual. It is to analogous causes that we must attribute the continued use of stone instruments in the religious ceremonies of peoples who are acquainted with iron and use it in ordinary life. In conclusion, they smeared the idols and the doors of the temples with the blood of the victims in order to appease the gods.[3]

All this is sufficiently crude and material, and rests upon the same premises as those which drove the Mexicans to the frightful excesses which I have previously described. But humanity was far less outraged in the Peruvian than in the Mexican religion. Gar-

---

[1] *Acosta*, ibid.; *Arriaga*, pp. 24—27 (cf. *Ternaux-Compans*, Vol. XVII. pp. 15, 16); *Prescott*, Bk. i. chap. iii.

[2] *Velasco*, Lib. ii. § 4, sec. 20.   [3] *Acosta*, ibid.; *Arriaga*, ibid.

cilasso deceives himself, or is attempting to deceive
his readers, when he gives his ancestors, the Incas,
the honour of having put an end to human sacrifices.[1]
It is certain that in the religion of Pachacamac more
especially this kind of sacrifice was frequent, and for
that matter we know that it was universal in the primitive epochs. All that we can allow to the descendant
of the Incas is, that they did not encourage, and were
rather disposed to restrain, human sacrifice. But for
all that, when the reigning Inca was ill, they sacrificed
one of his sons to the Sun, and prayed him to accept
the substitution of the son for the father. At certain
feasts a young infant was immolated. Others were
sacrificed to the subterranean spirits when a new Inca
was enthroned. To the same category we must attach
the custom which enjoined upon wives, especially
those of the Incas, the duty of burying themselves
alive on the death of their husbands. It is asserted
that when Huayna Capac died, a thousand members
of his household incurred a voluntary death that they
might go with him to serve him. The widows, however, were not compelled to take this step, and we
know that the Incas had organized the support of
widows without resources. But public opinion was
not favourable to those who refused to follow their

[1] *Garcilasso,* Lib. i. cap. xi., Lib. ii. cap. xviii., Lib. iv. cap. xv., and
elsewhere (pp. 6, &c., in Rycaut, who omits some of the passages).

husbands to the tomb. It was regarded as a species of infidelity.[1] We see, however, from other well-established facts, that the Peruvian religion had been gradually softened. In Peru, as in China, instead of the living beings that they used formerly to bury with the dead, they now placed statuettes of men and women with him in his tomb to represent his wives and his servants.[2]

We must also mention those "columns of the Sun" which appear never to have been absent in countries dominated by a solar worship. We have already seen them in Central America and in Mexico, and we also find them in Egypt, in Syria, in Asia Minor, in Palestine, at Carthage and elsewhere. In these columns the idea of fertilization is associated with that of the pleasure the Sun must feel in tracing out their shadows as he caresses their faces and summits with his rays. The earliest quadrants were traced at the foot of these columns. In Peru, they were levelled at the top, and were regarded as "seats of the Sun," who loved to rest upon them. At the equinoxes and solstices they placed golden thrones upon them for him to sit upon.

---

[1] *Montesinos,* p. 121; *Acosta,* Lib. v. capp. v. xix. Lib. vi. cap. xxii.; *Prescott,* Bk. i. chaps. i. ii; *Garcilasso,* Lib. vi. cap. v.; *Acosta,* Lib. v. cap. vii.; *Velasco,* Lib. iii. § i. sec. 1.

[2] *Gomara,* p. 234 a. Cf. *Montesinos,* p. 68, and *Pöppig* in Ersch u. Gruber's "Encyklopädie," art. *Incas,* p. 287 b, note 35.

Those nearest to the equator were held in greatest veneration, because the shadows were shorter there than elsewhere, and the sun appeared to rest vertically upon them.[1]

Prayer, in the proper sense of the word, asserted its place but feebly in the Peruvian religion. But hymns to the Sun were chanted at the great festivals and by the people as they went to cultivate the lands of the Sun. Every strophe ended with the cry, *Hailly*, or "triumph." It was the Peruvian *Io Pæan*. These chants, as far as they are still known to us, have something soft and sad about them. The rule of the Incas, paternal indeed, but monotonous in the extreme, must have tended to produce melancholy. In 1555, a Spanish composer wrote a mass upon the themes of these indigenous airs. It was sung in chorus, and it is chiefly to it that we owe the preservation of these chants.[2]

But the grand form of religious demonstration among the Peruvians was the dance. They were very assiduous in this form of devotion, and indeed we know what a large place the earliest of the arts occupied in the primitive religions generally. The dance

---

[1] *Garcilasso*, Lib. ii. capp. xxii. xxiii. (pp. 43, 44, in Rycaut); *Prescott*, Bk. i. chap. iv.; *Acosta*, Lib. vi. cap. iii.

[2] *Garcilasso*, Lib. v. cap. ii.; *Tschudi*, Vol. II. p. 382; "*Rivero y Tschudi :* Antiqüedades Peruanas: Viena, 1851." N. B. An English translation of this work by F. L. Hawks appeared at New York in 1853.

was the first and chief means adopted by pre-historic humanity of entering into active union with the deity adored. The first idea was to imitate the measured movements of the god, or at any rate what were supposed to be such. Afterwards, this fundamental motive was more or less forgotten; but the rite remained in force, like so many other religious forms which tradition and habit sustained even when the spirit was gone. In Peru, this tradition was still full of life. The name of the principal Peruvian festivals, *Raymi*, signifies "dance." The performances were so animated, that the dancers seemed to the Europeans to be out of their senses. It is noteworthy that the Incas themselves took no part in these violent dances, but had an "Incas' dance" of their own, which was grave and measured.[1]

There were four great official festivals in the year, coinciding with the equinoxes and the solstices. The first was the festival of the Winter solstice, which fell in June. It was the *Raymi*, or festival *par excellence*, the *Citoc Raymi*, the feast of the diminished and (henceforth) growing Sun. It lasted nine days, the first three of which were given up to fasting. On the morning of the great day, a grand procession, led by the reigning Inca and his family, followed by the

---

[1] *Velasco,* Lib. ii. § 5, secc. 4, 17 (Ternaux-Compans, Vol. XVIII. pp. 137, 148-9); *Külb,* l. c. p. 190.

nobles and the people, proceeded, with insignia, banners and symbolic masks, towards the place of the dawn and the rising Sun. When the luminary appeared, the crowd fell to the earth and threw him kisses. The Inca presented the sacred beverage to the Sun, drank some of it himself, and passed it on to his suite. This was a sort of solar communion. Then they went to the temple of the Sun to sacrifice a black llama there. After this, they kindled the new fire by means of the concave mirror, and slaughtered a number of llamas, representing the Sun's present to the people. The pieces were distributed to the families, where they were eaten with the sacred cakes prepared by the Virgins of the Sun. This was the second act of communion with the luminary to whom the day was sacred. The remaining days of the festival were passed in rejoicings, when the people seem to have made themselves ample amends for the fast with which they had begun.[1]

The second great festival, that of Spring, which fell in September, was the *Citua Raymi*, the feast of Purification. But do not attach any essentially moral significance to the idea of purification. The object in view was to purify the territory from all influences hostile to the health, security and prosperity of the inhabitants. Ball-shaped cakes were eaten on this

[1] *Garcilasso,* Lib. vi. capp. xx.—xxii.; *Prescott,* Bk. i. chap. iii.

occasion, in which was mixed the blood of victims or of young children, who were not slaughtered, however, but bled above the nose, which is evidence of a previous custom of far greater ferocity, and of the gradual softening of the Peruvian ritual. With this bread the people rubbed their bodies all over, and the doors of their houses likewise. Then, a little before sunset, a very strange ceremony was performed. An Inca, clad in precious armour and lance in hand, descended from the fortress of Cuzco, followed by four relatives whom the Sun had specially charged with the task of chasing away by open force all the maladies from the city and its environs. They traversed the chief streets of Cuzco at full speed, amid the acclamations of the inhabitants, and then surrendered their lances to others, who were relieved in their turn, till the limits of the ancient state of Cuzco were reached. There the lances were fixed in the ground, as so many talismans against evil influences. At night there was a great torchlight procession, at the close of which the torches were hurled into the river, and thus the evil spirits of the night were expelled, as those of the day had been by the lancers of the Sun.[1] Observe that in Africa, amongst the Blacks, a kind of " chase of the evil spirits" is practised (though accom-

[1] *Acosta*, Lib. v. cap. xxviii. [wrongly numbered xxvii. in the original edition]; *Garcilasso*, Lib. vii. capp. vi. viii.

panied with far fewer ceremonies than in Peru), in which the inhabitants of a village, armed with sticks and uttering formulæ of exorcism, expel the evil spirits from their houses and from their streets, and pursue them into the desert or the interior of a forest. But notice here, again, with what art the Incas had contrived to turn an old superstition to account in the interests of their own prestige. If maladies did not decimate the people of Cuzco, it was to their Incas that they owed their safety.

The third great festival, the Aymorai, which fell in May, celebrated the Harvest. A statue was constructed out of grains of corn glued together, and was adored under the name of *Pirrhua*, which in this case may well be a contraction of Viracocha, the god of fertilizing moisture. On this occasion a number of sacrifices were made at home by the householders.[1]

The fourth great feast fell in December. It was the *Copac Raymi*, the festival of power, in which the god of thunder was the object of a special worship by the side of the Sun. On this occasion the young Incas, after fasts, tournaments and other tests, received the investiture of manhood by having their ears pierced, and receiving a scarf, an axe and a crown of flowers. The young Curacas of the same age were also admitted to the privileges and duties of their rank, and shared

[1] *Acosta*, ibid.

with the Inca the sacred bread in token of indissolu-
ɔle communion with him.[1]

There were also a number of other and less import-
ɪnt feasts.   Each month had one of its own.   Then
there were occasional feasts, to celebrate the triumphal
return of a victorious Inca for example, or when the
tournaments of the young nobles, to which a religious
value was attached, took place, or when silent processions lasting a day and night, and followed by dances,
were instituted to avert threatening calamities, and so
forth.[2]   In Peru, as in so many other regions, eclipses
were the subject of great terror.   The eclipses of the
Sun were attributed to his own anger, those of the
Moon to an illness caused by the attack of an evil
spirit, to frighten which away and put it to flight a
hideous yelling was raised.[3]

There were sorcerers in Peru as everywhere else;
but in Peru too, as everywhere else where a priesthood has acquired a regular organization and made its
authority respected, sorcery was hardly resorted to
save by the lower classes.[4]   In fact, the sorcerer is the
priest of backward tribes, and the priest is the devel-

---

[1] *Acosta*, ibid. ; *Garcilasso*, Lib. vi. capp. xxiv.—xxvii.

[2] Cf. *Acosta*, ibid. ; *Velasco*, Lib. ii. § 5.

[3] *Gomara*, p. 233 b; *Garcilasso*, Lib. ii. cap. xxiii.; cf. *Montesinos*,
pp. 67, 68.

[4] *Balboa*, pp. 29, 30.

oped sorcerer. By his superior knowledge, by the more stable guarantees which he can give as the member of an imposing organization, by the nature of the religion of which he is the organ, and which raises him above the incoherent puerilities of animism, the priest eclipses the sorcerer and relegates him to the lower strata of society, which is just where his own titles to superiority are least appreciated. The sorcerer sinks in proportion as the priest rises.[1] For the rest, the official priesthood had its own diviners, who could foretel the future, the *Huacarimachi,* or "they who make the gods speak." The oracles of the valley of Rimac or Lima were much frequented; and, moreover, the Peruvians, like so many peoples of the Old World, thought that they could read the future in the entrails of the victims offered in sacrifice.[2] This widespread belief rests on the idea that immolation unites the victim so closely to the deity that it enters into communion with his thoughts and intentions, so that its heart, liver, and all other organs supposed to be affected by mental and moral dispositions, receive the impress of the divine prevision. Is it not passing strange, Gentlemen, that this mode of divination, which appears so absurd to us, which has no rational basis whatever, which rests on a singularly subtle con-

---

[1] Cf. *Arriga,* pp. 17—23, and *passim* (Ternaux-Compans, Vol. XVII. p. 15).   [2] See *Prescott,* ibid.

ception of the relations between the creature sacrificed and the being to whom it is offered, has secured the prolonged confidence of the peoples of the Old World, and appears again in Peru, where it cannot have been imitated from any one?

II.

It has been asked whether the native religion of Peru rested any system of elevated morals on its fundamental principles. Gentlemen, I am persuaded that religion and morals unite together and inter-penetrate each other in the higher regions of thought and life. Perhaps the most distinct result of our Christian education is the full comprehension of the fact that what is moral is religious, and that immo-rality cannot on any pretext be allowed as legiti-mately religious. But we must certainly yield to the overwhelming evidence that in the lower stages of religion this union of the two sisters is present only in germ. Religion, still quite selfish in its charac-ter, pursues its own way and seeks its own satisfac-tions independently of all moral considerations, and almost always lives in a state of separation from morality. We ought therefore to expect that in systems such as that of Peru—which have already risen much above the low level of the primitive reli-gions, but are still far below that of the higher ones

N

—we should find a certain religious ethic, a certain moral tendency in religion, but likewise all kinds of inconsistencies, and constant relapses towards the ancient separation of the two sisters. As a general rule, we may say that even where the Peruvian religion seems to undertake the elevation and protection of morals, it does so rather with a utilitarian and selfish view, than with any real purpose of sanctifying the heart and will.

Thus we have noted ceremonies which forcibly recall the Communion. But the great object in view was to secure to the communicants the safety and well-being that would result from their union with the Sun or his representatives. The moral idea occupies but a small place in this communion, though it is but right to add that the great social laws were placed under the patronage and sanction of the Sun, whose legislation the Incas were held responsible for enforcing. In the same way we find in Peru something that closely resembles baptism. From fifteen to twenty days after birth the child received its first name, after being plunged into water. But this purification had nothing to do with the ideas of sin and regeneration. It was but a form of exorcism, destined to secure the child from the evil spirits and their malign influences. Between the ages of ten and twelve, the child's definite name was con-

9

ferred. On this occasion his hair and nails were cut off, and offered to the Sun and the guardian spirits.[1] This represented the consecration of his person, but its main object was to secure him the protection of the divine power.

There was likewise a sacerdotal confession, but it was an institution of state and of police rather than a sacrament with a moral purpose. The great object was to discover all actions, whether voluntary or not, which might bring misfortune upon the state if not expiated by the appropriate penances and rites. The father confessors of Peru were inquisitors charged with the searching out of secret faults and the exaction of their avowal. A refusal to confess might provoke severe measures. A proof of the small influence of the moral element in the whole system of inquisition may be found in the fact that the priest relied on purely fortuitous tests in deciding whether or not to give absolution. For instance, he would take a pinch of maize grains, and if the number turned out to be even, he would declare the confession good, and give absolution, otherwise he would say the penitent must have concealed something, and would make him confess again.[2]

Cf *Velasco*, Lib. ii. § 3, secc. 4, 5.

[2] *Balboa*, p. 3; *Velasco*, Lib. ii. § 3, sec. 6; *Arriaga*, pp. 28, 29 (Ternaux-Compans, Vol. XVII. pp. 16, 17).

Our conviction that the Peruvian religion had but a very elementary moral significance, receives a final confirmation from the beliefs concerning the future life.

It is clear that no very definite ideas on this point had become generally established. In fact, we find amongst the Peruvians at the time of the conquest the underlying conceptions of the most widely severed peoples, all mingled together. Thus the common people of Peru, like all savages, thought of the future life as a continuation, pure and simple, of the present life. This explains the custom of burying all kinds of useful and desirable objects with the dead—giving him an emigrant's outfit, in short. The worship of ancestors is easily grafted upon this conception of the life beyond the grave. These ancestors may still succour, protect and inspire their descendants. I am assured at first hand that to this very day, and in spite of the efforts of the Catholic clergy, the worship of ancestors is still widely practised by the native population. There was not the least idea of a resurrection of the body. If the corpse was preserved, especially in the case of departed Incas, it was because the Peruvians believed that the soul which had left it still retained a marked predilection for its ancient abode and liked to return to it from time to time; and also because they attributed magic virtues to the remains thus preserved. No idea of recompense is as yet associated with this purely animistic and primitive conception of the life beyond the tomb.[1]

Amongst the higher classes, the ideas entertained on this same subject had become a little less naive. The Incas were supposed to be transported to the mansion of the Sun, their father, where they still lived together as his family. The Curacas or nobles would either follow them there, or would still live under the earth beneath the sceptre of the god of the dead, Supay, the Hades or Pluto of the Peruvian mythology. Do not identify this deity with a Satan or Ahriman of any kind. He was not a wicked, but rather a sinister god, the conception of whom could wake no joyous or even serene emotions. He was a voracious deity, of insatiable appetite. At Quito, at any rate before the conquest of the country by the Incas, a hundred children were sacrificed to him every year. There is no idea of positive suffering inflicted on the wicked under his direction. But the subterranean abode is gloomy and dismal like the place of shades in the Odyssey. Exceptional considerations of birth, rank or valour in war, determine the passage of chosen souls to heaven, where their lot will of course be far more brilliant and

[1] Cf. *Tschudi* Vol. II. pp. 353-6, 397-8.

happy than that of the souls that remain in the subterranean regions. Thus the aristocratic point of
view, barely modified by the high importance attributed to the warlike virtues, still dominates the
ideas of a future life in ancient Peru, as in Mexico,
in Polynesia and in Africa. This is a final proof
that the moral element was but feebly present in
the ancient Peruvian religion. For wherever a clear
and definite belief in a conscious life beyond the
grave is united to a sense of the religious character
of morality, it is likewise held, by an obvious connection of ideas, that the lot of departed souls will
depend completely upon their moral condition, without distinction of birth or rank.[1]

This Peruvian religion, then, in spite of its elevation
and refinement in some respects, forcibly reminds us
of the walls of its own temples, all plated with gold,
but covered in with straw, and poor and unvaried in
architecture. A monotonous, unformed, gloomy spirit
seems to pervade the whole institution, in spite of its
brilliant exterior. The air of the convent broods over
it. Those thousands of functionaries who spent their
lives in superintending the furniture, the dress, the

---

[1] *Acosta*, Lib. v. capp. vi. vii.; *Velasco*, Lib. ii. ∤ 3, sec. 3.;
Arriaga, p. 15 (cf. Ternaux-Compans, Vol. XVII. p. 14); *Garcilasso*, Lib. ii. capp. ii. (Supay), vii. (omitted by Rycaut); *Prescott*, Bk.
i. chap. iii.

work, the very cookery, of the families under their charge, and inflicting corporal chastisement on those whom they surprised in a fault, might succeed in forming a correct and regular society, drilled like the bees in a hive, might form a nation of submissive slaves, but could never make a nation of *men;* and this is the deep cause that explains the irremediable collapse of this Peruvian society under the vigorous blows of a handful of unscrupulous Spaniards. It was a skilfully constructed machine, which worked like a chronometer; but when once the mainspring was broken, all was over.

It is no part of our task to tell the story of the conversion of the natives to Roman Catholic Christianity. It was comparatively easily effected. The fall of the Incas was a mortal blow to the religious, no less than to the political, edifice in which they were the keystone of the arch. It was evident that the Sun had been unable or unwilling to protect his children. The conqueror imposed his religion on Peru, as on Mexico, by open force; and the Spanish Inquisition, though not giving rise to such numerous and terrible spectacles in the former as in the latter country, yet carried out its work of terror and oppression there too. The result was that peculiar character of the Catholicism of the natives of Peru which strikes every traveller, and consists in a kind of timid and superstitious submission, without confidence and without zeal, associated with the obstinate preservation of customs which mount back to the former religious régime, and with memories of the golden age of the Inca rule under which their ancestors were obliged to live, but which has gone to return no more.

III.

And now it only remains for us to draw the inferences and conclusions suggested by our examination of the ancient religions of Mexico and Peru, so closely associated with the remarkable though imperfect civilizations to which the two 'nations had attained.

We have not stayed to discuss the hypotheses that have so often been put forward, to attach these religions and civilizations to some immigration from the Old World. The fact is that all these attempts rest on the arbitrary selection of some few traits of resemblance, on which exclusive stress is laid, to the neglect of still more characteristic differences. The best proof that the work of affiliation has been abortive, in spite of the high authority of some of the names that have been lent to it, may be found in the fact that every possible nation of the Old World has in its turn been selected as the true parent of the Peruvians and Mexicans. The Carthaginians, the Greeks, the Chinese, the Hindus, the Buddhists of India and China, the Romans, even the Celts and the Chaldeans, have been put forward one after the other. Nay, the English themselves have been tried! There is a gratifying legend which brings the story of Manco Capac and Mama Ogllo into connection with the results of the shipwreck of an *Englishman*, whose national name was transformed into *Inga Man*, which again, in conjunction with *Cocapac*, the name of the father of the native wife whom the Englishman had taken to himself, made *Inca Manco Capac!* The sequel is obvious. The two fair-skinned children that sprang from this union were of course the founders of the Inca family and the state of Cuzco.[1] I need not tell you that all this will not bear a moment's examination. Everything shows that the civilizations and religions of Mexico and Peru are autochthonous, springing from the soil itself.

There is surely something very strange in this passion for localizing all origins at some single point of the globe. Why not admit that what took place there may have taken place elsewhere also, that the same concourse of events which called forth such and such a result in a certain given place may have

---

[1] Compare *W. B. Stevenson*, "A Historical and Descriptive Narrative of Twenty Years' Residence in South America:" London, 1825, Vol. I. pp. 394 sqq.

been reproduced somewhere else, and consequently given rise to identical or closely analogous results there too? Does not our own experience teach us that the contact of a civilized with an uncivilized people is not enough in itself to ensure the adoption by the latter of the civilization that is brought to it? It is the exception, not the rule, for the Redskin, the Kafir, the Australian or the Papuan, to become civilized. Civilization can only be handed on if the invaded race possesses a special disposition and aptitude for civilized life; and this aptitude may have existed to such a degree as to be capable of independent development in the New World as we know it did in the Old; and if there were centres of such nascent civilization in Central America, in Mexico and in Peru, it is absolutely superfluous to search elsewhere than in America itself for the origins of American civilization.

But the mistake into which so many historians and travellers have fallen is explained, to a certain extent, by the fact that, in examining the beliefs, the monuments and the customs of Peru and Mexico, we come upon phenomena at every moment which are identical with or analogous to something we have observed in the Old World. The temples, with their successive terraces, remind us of ancient Chaldea, and the hieroglyphics of ancient Egypt.

The convents recal the Indian and Chinese Buddhism. The cruel and bloody sacrifices and the preponderance of the Sun-worship have a Semitic tinge. There are myths and curious resemblances of words which wake thoughts of Hellenic civilization; and sacerdotal castes and sacrificial rites which bring us round to the Celts! Nay, are there not even beliefs as to the arrival or return of a deity who will restore order and avenge outraged justice, round which there breathes a kind of Messianic air? So much so, indeed, that I must add to the list of supposed ancestors of American civilization the ten lost tribes of Israel, who must have fled from the yoke of their Ninevite oppressors right across Asia into America! The partizans of this ingenious hypothesis have, it is true, forgotten to inquire how far these Israelites of the North, whose enthusiasm for the house of Judah was, to say the least of it, decidedly subdued, had ever heard of the Messianic hopes at all!

The real result of all these wild speculations, however, is to bring out the fact very clearly, that in the native religions of Mexico, of Central America and of Peru, we find a number of traits united which are scattered amongst the most celebrated religions of our own ancient world; so that this new and well-defined region gives us a precious opportunity of testing the value of the explanations of religious ideas and practices deduced from the comparative study of religions.

Let us take the question of sacrifice, for instance. In both religions sacrifice is frequent, often cruel,— in Mexico even frightful. But it is easy to trace the original idea that inspired it. It is by no means the sense of guilt, or the idea that the culprit, terrified by the account that he must render to the divine justice, can transfer to a victim the penalty he has himself incurred. It is simply the idea that by offering the gods the things they like—that is to say, whatever will satisfy and gratify their senses —it is possible to secure their goodwill, their protection and their favour, while at the same time disarming their wrath, if need be, and appeasing their dangerous appetites. It is only at a later stage that the extreme importance attributed to this rite, the very essence of the worship rendered to the gods, leads to the association of mystic and ultimately of moral ideas with the circumstance of the pain inseparably connected with sacrifice. And when this stage is reached, men will either refine upon the suffering with frantic intensity, as they did in Mexico, or, if the sentiment of humanity has made itself felt in religion, as was the case in Peru and in the special worship of Quetzalcoatl, they will try to restrain the number and mitigate

the horror of the human sacrifices, while still in-
flexibly maintaining the principle they involve.

Again: there is not the smallest trace of an earlier
monotheism preceding the polytheism of either the
one or the other nation. On the other hand, we may
trace in both alike three stages of religious faith super-
imposed, so to speak, one upon the other. At the
bottom of all still lies the religion that we find to-day
amongst peoples that are strangers to all civilization.
It is an incoherent and confused jumble of nature-
worship and of animism or the worship of spirits, but
especially the latter; for the primitive nature-worship
has been developed, enlarged and more or less organized, on a higher level, whereas animism has remained
what it was. The spirits of nature, which may often
be anonymous—spirits of forests, of plants, of rocks,
of waters, of animals, generally with the addition of
the spirits of ancestors—make up a confused and inor-
ganic mass that may assume almost any form. Fetichism is not the base, as it has been called, but the consequence and application of this animistic view. It is
enough to secure adoration for any worthless object,
natural or artificial, if it strikes the ignorant imagination forcibly enough to induce the belief that it is the
residence of a spirit. Magic, founded on the pretension of certain individuals to stand in special relations with the spirits, equips the priesthood of this

lowest stage.　But above this, through the action of the higher minds amongst the people, nature-worship develops itself into the adoration of the most important, most general and most imposing phenomena of nature.　In the tropical countries, at once warm and fertile, it is the Sun that reigns supreme, though not without leaving a very exalted place to other phenomena, such as wind, rain, vegetation and so on, personified as so many special deities.　But in all this there is no indication of an antecedent and primitive monotheism.　It is quite true that each one of these deities receives in his turn epithets which seem to attribute omnipotence to him and to make him the sole creator.　But this is the case in all polytheistic systems, whether in Greece, Persia, and India, or in Mexico and Peru.　It only proves that when man worships, he never limits the homage he renders to the object of his adoration; but if he is a polytheist, he has no scruple in attributing the same omnipotence to each of his gods in turn.　It is much the same with the worthy curés in our rural districts, whose sermons systematically exalt the saint of the day, whoever he may be, to the chief place in Paradise!　And here in Mexico and in Peru, as in Greece and in India, we observe the ever growing tendency towards *anthropomorphism*, transforming into men, of enormous strength, stature and power, those natural phenomena which at the earlier stage were rather assimilated to animals. Uitzilopochtli still bears the traces of his ancient nature as a humming-bird, and Tezcatlipoca of the time when he was no more than a celestial tapir. Their cultus, like their functions in the order of nature, must be regular and subject to fixed rules, And thus the priesthood, organized and regulated in its turn, emerges from the earlier stage of sorcery, and becomes a great institution to protect and foster the nascent civilization. The third stage was not actually reached in ancient Mexico and Peru. One can but divine its beginnings in the mysterious priesthood of Quetzalcoatl, or trace it in the traditions of the philosopher king of Tezcuco, and the sceptical Incas of whom Garcilasso and others tell us. In such traits as these we may discover a certain dissatisfaction with the established polytheism, striving to raise itself higher in the direction of a spiritual monotheism. But this tendency is obviously the last term of the evolution, and in no sense its first.

The history of the temple in Mexico and Peru suggests similar reflections. Its point of departure is the altar, and not the tomb,—the altar on which, as on a sacred table, the flesh destined for their food was placed before the gods. Little by little, as the developed and organized nature-worship substitutes gods of imposing might and greatness for the contemptible deities of the period when nature-worship and animism were confounded together, these altars assumed huge and at last gigantic proportions ; and in Mexico, except in the case of Quetzalcoatl, there the development stopped, save that a little chapel, destined to serve as the abode of the national gods, was reared on the summit. Peru passes through the same phases, but goes further. There the surmounting chapel grows, assumes vast dimensions, and ends by embracing the altar itself, of which at first it was but an adjunct.

The two religions alike exhibit an initial penetration of religion by the moral idea. They are at bottom two theocracies, the laws and institutions of which rest upon the gods themselves, though the theocratic form is far more prominent in Peru than in Mexico. They share the advantages of a theocracy for a nascent civilization, and its disadvantages for one that has already reached a certain development. It was the theocratic and sacerdotal conception that maintained and enforced the religious butchery of which you have heard in Mexico, and which transformed Peru into one enormous convent, where no one had any will or any initiative of his own. For the same reason, asceticism, the principle that confuses, through an illusion we can easily understand, the moral act itself with the suffering that accompanies it, shows itself in both religions, but especially in that of Mexico ; and convents that startle us by their resemblance to those of Buddhism and Christianity rise in either realm. But this mutual interpenetration of the religious and moral ideas is still quite rudimentary. The prevailing tone of the religion is given by the self-seeking and purely calculating principle, aiming no doubt at a certain mystic satisfaction (for at every stage of religion this moving principle has been most powerful and fruitful), but likewise seeking material advantages without any scruple as to the means; and those monstrous forms of transubstantiation which the Mexican thought he was bringing about when he ate of the same human flesh which he offered to his gods, are typical of the period in which religion pursued its purpose of union with the deity, regardless of the protests of the moral sense and of humanity.

It was reserved for the higher religions, and especially for that of which our Bible is the monument, to realize the intimate alliance of the religious and moral sentiments, — that priceless alliance, without which morals remain for the most part almost barren, and religion falls into monstrous aberrations. That the roots of religion pierce to the very cradles of humanity, may now be taken as demonstrated. Its principle is found in the necessity we feel of surmounting the uncertainties and the limitations of destiny, by attaching ourselves individually to the loftier Spirit revealed by nature outside us and within; and this

o

principle has always remained the same; nor am I
one of those who hold that we must now renounce it
in the name of philosophy and science. For neither
philosophy nor science can make us other than
the poor creatures we are, with an unquenchable
thirst for blessedness and life, yet constantly broken,
crushed at every moment, by the very elements on the
bosom of which we are forced to live. Philosophy
and science may guide religion, may reveal its true
object in ever-growing purity, may cleanse it from
the pollutions in which ignorance and sin still plunge
it, but they cannot replace and they cannot destroy it.
There is a Dutch proverb, the profundity of which it
would be difficult to exaggerate, " De natuur gaat
boven de leer "—*Nature is too strong for doctrine.*
The evolutions of philosophy may seem to make the
heavens void, and inspire man with the idea that all is
over with the poetic or terrific visions that rocked the
cradle of his infancy. But stay! Nature, human
nature, is still there; and under the impulse of the
indestructible thirst for religion, human nature renews
her efforts, looks deeper and looks higher, and finds
her God once more.

Jérusalem renait plus brilliante et plus belle.

But let not this conclusion, confirmed as it seems
to me by the whole history of religion, prevent our

boldly declaring how much that is small, puerile, often even immoral and deplorable, there is in the religious past of humanity. It is no otherwise with art, with legislation, with science herself, with all that constitutes the privilege, the power, the joy of our race. It is just the knowledge of these aberrations which should serve to keep us from falling back into the errors and false principles of which they were the consequence. And in this respect the study of the religions of ancient Mexico and Peru is profoundly instructive. It teaches us that there is a principle, bordering closely upon that of religion itself, which must serve as the torch to guide the religious idea in its development—not to supplant it, but to direct it to the true path. It is the principle of humanity. The truer a religion is, the more absolute the homage it will render to the principle of humanity, and the more will he who lives by its light feel himself impelled to goodness, loving and loved, trustful and free. The last word of religious history is, that there exists an affinity, a mysterious relationship, between our spirit and the Spirit of the universe; that this nobility of human nature embraces in itself all the promises, all the hopes, all the latent perfections, all the infinite ideals of the future; that, in spite of all appearances to the contrary, the Supreme Will is good to each one of the beings which it summons and draws to itself; and that man, in spite of his errors, his failures, his corruptions, his miseries, was never wrong in following the sacred instinct that raised him slowly from the mire, was always right in renewing his efforts, so constant, so toilsome—often, too, so woful—to mount the rounds.

De cette échelle d'or qui va se perdre en Dieu.

And now, Ladies and Gentlemen, it only remains for me to bid you farewell, while giving you my warmest thanks for the perseverance, the encouragement and the sympathy, with which you have supported me. The reception you have given me has touched me deeply, and my stay in 1884 in your imposing and splendid capital will always remain amongst the most prized and the pleasantest recollections of my life. You have been good enough to pardon my linguistic infirmity. You have spared from your business or pleasure the time needed to listen to a stranger, who has come to speak to you of matters having no direct utility, and of purely historical and theoretical interest. This is far more to your honour than to mine. I thank you, but at the same time I congratulate you; for it is a trait in the nobleness in our human nature to be able thus to snatch ourselves from the vulgar pre-occupations of life, to contemplate the truth on those serene heights where it reveals itself to all who seek it with an upright heart. Cease not to love these noble studies, which touch upon all that is most exalted and most precious in us! If we search history for light in politics and the higher interests of our fatherlands, and learn thereby to understand, to appreciate, to love them more, let us turn to history no less for light on the path which we must tread in that order of sublime realities, necessities and aspirations, in which the soul of each one of us becomes a temple and a sanctuary, lying open to the Eternal Spirit that fills the universe.

And now to the Eternal, the Invisible, to Him whose name we can but stammer, whose infinite perfections we can but feel after, be rendered all our homage and our hearts!

THE END.